"You said you _____
weren't really going to have sex on his desk, but he
reveled in the regret in her eyes that she couldn't hide
in spite of her scowl.

"You're being outrageous."

"Good."

"Stop. Now," she said firmly.

Okay, he'd pushed her far enough for today, but he
could see that while their love for each other might
have burned out, their passion still had plenty of fire
left.

He buttoned his shirt again and tucked in the tails.
"Spoilsport."

She brushed papers into a stack. "The pilot's waiting."

"Damn waste of an empty desk," he said with a smile.

* * *

One Good Cowboy is part of
the Diamonds in the Rough trilogy:

The McNair cousins must pass their grandmother's tests
to inherit their fortune—and find true love!

* * *

If you're on Twitter,
tell us what you think of Harlequin Desire!
#harlequindesire

Dear Reader,

I've long been a fan of John Wayne's Western movies! I love Saturday evening marathon movie sessions watching "The Duke" at his finest, riding the range with a strong back and a strong code of ethics. Dreamy sigh! What a hero!

Those movies made me long to write a cowboy hero of my own—but in modern day times, of course. From that came my idea for the McNair family and the Diamonds in the Rough trilogy. I hope you enjoy Stone's story and will be on the lookout for follow-up books on his cousins—Alex and Amie.

Thank you so much for picking up *One Good Cowboy*. Yee-haw and happy reading!

Cheers,
Cathy

Catherine Mann
USA TODAY bestselling author
RWA award winner
Website: CatherineMann.com
Facebook: Facebook.com/CatherineMannAuthor
Twitter: Twitter.com/#!/CatherineMann1
Pinterest: Pinterest.com/CatherineMann/

ONE GOOD COWBOY

—

CATHERINE MANN

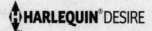
HARLEQUIN® DESIRE

Recycling programs
for this product may
not exist in your area.

ISBN-13: 978-0-373-73306-4

ONE GOOD COWBOY

Printed in U.S.A.

Books by Catherine Mann

Harlequin Desire

Silhouette Desire

*The Landis Brothers
ΔRich, Rugged & Royal
**The Alpha Brotherhood
ΩDiamonds in the Rough

Other titles by this author available in ebook format.

CATHERINE MANN

USA TODAY bestselling author Catherine Mann lives on a sunny Florida beach with her flyboy husband and their four children. With more than forty books in print in over twenty countries, she has also celebrated wins for both a RITA® Award and a Booksellers' Best Award. Catherine enjoys chatting with readers online—thanks to the wonders of the internet, which allows her to network with her laptop by the water! Contact Catherine through her website, www.catherinemann.com, find her on Facebook and Twitter (@CatherineMann1) or reach her by snail mail at P.O. Box 6065, Navarre, FL 32566.

To my husband, Rob, always my hero.

One

"Gentlemen, never forget the importance of protecting your family jewels."

Unfazed by his grandmother's outrageous comment, Stone McNair ducked low as his horse sailed under a branch and over a creek. Gran prided herself on being the unconventional matriarch of a major jewelry design empire, and her mocking jab carried on the wind as Stone raced with his cousin.

Alex pulled up alongside him, neck and neck with Stone's quarter horse. Hooves chewed at the earth, deftly dodging the roots of a cypress tree, spewing turf into the creek.

Even as he raced, Stone soaked in the scents and sounds of home—the squeak of the saddle, the whistle of the wind through the pines. Churned earth and bluebonnets waving in the wind released a fragrance every bit as intoxicating as the first whiff of a freshly opened bottle of Glenfiddich whiskey.

This corner of land outside of Fort Worth, Texas, had belonged to the McNairs for generations, their homestead as they built a business empire. His blood hummed when he rode the ranch. Ownership had branded itself into his DNA as tangibly as the symbol of the Hidden

Gem Ranch that had been branded onto his quarter horse's flank.

Outings on the ranch with his grandmother and his twin cousins were few and far between these days, given their hectic work schedules. He wasn't sure why Gran had called this little reunion and impromptu race, but it had to be something important for her to resort to pulling them all away from the McNair Empire.

His other cousin, Amie, galloped alongside Stone, her laughter full and uninhibited. "How're the family jewels holding up?"

Without waiting for an answer, Amie urged her Arabian ahead, her McNair-black hair trailing behind her just like when she'd been ten instead of thirty. Rides with their grandmother had been a regular occurrence when they were children, then less and less frequent as they grew older and went their separate ways. None of them had hesitated when the family matriarch insisted on an impromptu gathering. Stone owed his grandmother. She'd been his safe haven every time his druggy mother went on a binge or checked into rehab.

Again.

Damn straight, he owed his grandmother a debt he couldn't repay. She'd been there from day one, an aggressive advocate in getting the best care possible to detox her crack baby grandson. Gran had paid for her daughter to enter detox programs again and again with little success. Year after year, Gran had been as constant as the land they called home—for his cousins, too.

And she'd given each one of them a role to play. Alex managed the family lands—Hidden Gem Ranch, which operated as a bed-and-breakfast hobby ranch for the rich and famous. Stone managed the family jewelry design house and stores. Diamonds in the Rough featured high-end rustic designs, from rodeo belt buckles and stylized bolos to Aztec jewelry, all highly sought after around the country. If everything went according to plan, he intended to expand Diamonds in the Rough with international offices in London and Milan, making the big announcement at a wild mustang fund-raiser this fall. And Amie—a gemologist—was already working on designs for new pieces to meet the expected increase in demand.

Yes, the world was finally coming back together for him. After his broken engagement knocked him for a loop seven months ago…

But he didn't want to think about Johanna. Not today. Not ever, if he could avoid it. Although that was tough to accomplish, since Johanna worked for Hidden Gem Stables as a vet tech. He'd missed her this morning when they'd saddled up. Would he bump into her after his ride?

The possibility filled him with frustration—and an unwanted boot in the libido.

Gran slowed her favorite palomino, Goldie, to a trot near the pond where they'd played as kids. Apparently race time was over. Maybe now she would explain the reason for this surprise get-together.

Stone stroked along Copper's neck as the horse dipped his head to drink. "So, Gran, care to enlighten us on the reason for this family meeting?"

His cousins drew up along either side of her.

She shifted in the saddle, her head regal with a long gray braid trailing down her stiff spine. "The time has come for me to decide who will take over the reins of the McNair holdings."

Stone's grip tightened on the pommel. "You're not actually considering retiring."

"No, dear…" Gran paused, drawing in a shaky breath at odds with her usual steel. "The doctor has told me it's time to get my affairs in order."

Her words knocked the wind out of him as fully as the first time he'd been thrown from a horse. He couldn't envision a world without the indomitable Mariah McNair.

Amie reached across to touch her grandmother's arm lightly, as much contact as could be made without everyone dismounting, and Gran didn't show any signs of leaving the saddle. Which was probably the reason their grandmother had chosen this way to make her announcement.

"Gran, what exactly did the doctor say?"

Alex patted Gran's other shoulder, he and his sister protecting her like bookends. They always had.

Amie's and Alex's childhoods had been more stable than Stone's, with parents and a home of their own. As a kid, Stone had dreamed of stepping into their house and becoming a sibling rather than a cousin. Once he'd even overheard his grandmother suggest that very arrangement. But Amethyst and Alexandrite's mother made it clear that she could handle only her twins. Another child would be too much to juggle between obligations to her daughter's pageants and her son's rodeos.

In one fell swoop, Stone had realized that while his family loved him, no one wanted him—not his mother, his aunt or his grandmother. They were all looking for some way to shuffle him off. Except Gran hadn't bailed. She'd taken him on regardless. He respected and loved her all the more for that.

Mariah patted each twin on the cheek and smiled sadly at Stone since he held himself apart. "It's inoperable brain cancer."

His throat closed up tight. Amie gasped, blinking fast but a tear still escaped.

Their grandmother shook her head. "None of that emotional stuff. I've never had much patience for tears. I want optimism. Doctors are hopeful treatment can reduce the size of the tumor. That could give me years instead of months."

Months?

Damn it.

The wind got knocked out of him all over again. More than once, Stone had been called a charmer with a stone-cold heart. But that heart ached right now at the thought of anything happening to his grandmother.

Shrugging, Mariah leaned back in the saddle. "Still, even if the treatments help, I can't risk the tumor clouding my judgment. I won't put everything I've worked for at risk by waiting too long to make important decisions about Diamonds in the Rough and the Hidden Gem Ranch."

The family holdings meant everything to her. To all of them. It had never dawned on him until now that his grandmother—the major stockholder—might want to change the roles they all played to keep the empire rock-solid. He must be mistaken. Better to wait and hear her out rather than assume.

Amie wasn't so restrained, but then she never had been. "What have you decided?"

"I haven't," Mariah conceded. "Not yet, but I have a plan, which is why I asked you three to come riding with me today."

Alex, the quiet one of the bunch, frowned. "I'm not sure I understand."

"You'll each need to do something for me—" Mariah angled forward, forearm on the saddle horn "—something to help put my mind at ease about who to place in charge."

"You're testing us," Amie accused softly.

"Call it what you like." Gran was unapologetic, her jaw set. "But as it stands now, I'm not sold on any of you taking over."

That revelation stabbed pain clear through his already raw nerves.

Enough holding back. He was a man of action, and the urge to be in control of something, anything, roared through him. "What do you need me to do for you?"

"Stone, you need to find homes for all four of my dogs."

A fish plopped in the pond, the only sound breaking his stunned silence.

Finally, he asked, "You're joking, right? To lighten the mood."

"I'm serious. My pets are very important to me. You know that. They're family."

"It just seems a...strange test." Was the tumor already affecting her judgment?

His grandmother shook her head slowly. "The fact that you don't know how serious this is merely affirms my concerns. You need to prove to me you have the heart to run this company and possibly oversee the entire family portfolio."

She held him with her clear blue gaze, not even a whisper of confusion showing. Then she looked away, clicked her horse into motion and started back toward the main house, racing past the cabins vacationers rented.

Shaking off his daze, he followed her, riding along the split rail fence, his cousins behind him as they made their way home.

Home.

Some would call it a mansion—a rustic log ranch house with two wings. Their personal living quarters occupied one side, and the other side housed the lodge run by Alex. His cousin had expanded the place from a small bed-and-breakfast to a true hobby ranch, with everything from horseback riding to a spa, fishing and trail adventures…even poker games, saloon-style. They catered to a variety of people's needs, from vacations to weddings.

The gift store featured some of the McNair signature jewelry pieces, just a sampling from their flagship store in Fort Worth.

Alex was one helluva businessman in his own right. Gran could be serious about turning over majority control to him.

Or maybe she had someone else in mind. A total stranger. He couldn't even wrap his brain around that unthinkable possibility. His whole being was consumed with shock—and hell, yes, grief—not over the fact that he might lose the company but because he would lose Gran. A month or a year from now, he couldn't envision a world without her.

And he also couldn't deny her anything she needed to make her last days easier.

Stone urged his horse faster to catch her before she reached the stables.

"Okay, fine, Gran," he said as he pulled alongside

her, their horses' gaits in sync. "I can do that for you. I'll line up people to take, uh…" What the hell were their names? "Your dogs."

"There are four of them, in case you've forgotten that, as well as forgetting their names."

"The scruffy one's named Dorothy, right?"

Gran snorted almost as loudly as the horse. "Close. The dog looks like Toto, but her name is Pearl. The yellow lab is Gem, given to us by a friend. My precious Rottie that I adopted from a shelter is named Ruby. And my baby chi-weenie's name is Sterling."

Chi-what? Oh, right, a Chihuahua and dachshund. "What about your two cats?"

Surely he would get points for remembering there were two.

"Amie is keeping them."

She always was a suck-up.

"Then I'll keep the dogs. They can live with me." How much trouble could four dogs be? He had lots of help. He would find one of those doggy day cares.

"I said I wanted them to go to *good* homes."

He winced. "Of course you do."

"Homes approved of by an expert," she continued as she stopped her horse by the stables.

"An expert?" Hairs on the back of his neck rose with an impending sense of Karma about to bite him on the butt.

He didn't even have to look down the lengthy walkway between horse stalls to know Johanna Fletcher was striding toward them on long, lean legs that could have sold a million pairs of jeans. She usually wore a French braid to keep her wavy blond hair secure when she worked. His fingers twitched at the memory of sliding through that braid to unleash all those tawny strands around her bare shoulders.

What he wouldn't give to lose himself in her again, to forget about the thought of his grandmother's illness. Even if the best scenario played out, a couple of years wasn't enough.

For now, he would do whatever it took to keep Gran happy.

"Your expert?" he prodded.

"All adoptions must be approved by our ranch vet tech, Johanna Fletcher."

Of course.

His eyes slid to Johanna closing the gap between them as she went from stall to stall, horse to horse. Her face shuttered the instant she looked at him, whereas once she would have met him with a full-lipped smile, a slight gap between her front teeth. That endearing imperfection only enhanced her attractiveness. She was down-to-earth and sexy. He knew every inch of her intimately.

After all, she was his ex-fiancée.

The woman who had dumped him in no uncertain terms in front of all their friends at a major fund-raiser. A woman who now hated his guts and would like nothing more than to see his dreams go up in flames.

Stone McNair, the CEO in a business suit ruling the boardroom, commanded respect and awe. But Stone McNair, cowboy Casanova on a horse, was a charismatic charmer Johanna Fletcher had always been hard-pressed to resist.

Johanna tamped down the urge to fan herself as she stood just outside a horse stall and studied her former

lover out of the corner of her eyes. Damn it, he still
made her hot all over.

She busied herself with listening to a horse's heartbeat—or pretending to listen at least. The palomino
was fine, but she didn't want anyone thinking she was
still pining for Stone. Everyone from Fort Worth to Del
Rio knew her history with him. She didn't need to feed
them any fodder for gossip by drooling every time he
strutted into the stables.

Lord help her, that man knew how to strut.

Jeans hugged his thighs as he swung a leg over his
horse, boots hitting the ground with a thud that vibrated
clear through her even from twenty yards away. The sun
flashed off his belt buckle—a signature Diamonds in
the Rough design—bringing out the nuances of the pattern. Magnificent. Just like the man. All the McNairs
had charisma, but Stone was sinfully handsome, with
coal-black hair and ice-blue eyes right off some movie
poster. Sweat dotted his brow, giving his hair a hint of
a curl along the edges of his tan Stetson. She'd idolized him as a child. Fantasized about him as a teenager.

And as a woman? She'd fallen right in line with the
rest and let herself be swayed by his charms.

Never again.

Johanna turned her focus back to the next stall with
a quarter horse named Topaz, one of the more popular
rides for vacationers. She had a job to do and she was
darn lucky to work here after the scene she'd caused
during her breakup with Stone. But Mrs. McNair liked
her and kept her on. Johanna hadn't been able to resist
the opportunity to work with so many unique horses
in the best stable.

Her career was everything to her now, and she refused to put it in jeopardy. Her parents had sacrificed their life's savings to send her to the best schools so she had the educational foundation she needed to pursue her dreams. Although her parents were gone now after a fire in the trailer park, she owed them. Perhaps even more so to honor their memory. Her father's work here had brought her into the McNair world—brought her to Stone, even if their romance ultimately hadn't been able to withstand the wide social chasm between them.

She had no family, not even the promise of one she'd once harbored while engaged to Stone. She had her work, her horses. This was her life and her future.

Hooves clopped as Mariah and Stone passed off their rides to two stable hands. Johanna frowned. Even though the McNairs were wealthy, they usually unsaddled and rubbed down their horses themselves. Instead, the grandmother and grandson were walking directly toward her. Tingles pranced up and down her spine. Ignoring him would be impossible.

She hooked her stethoscope around her neck. Her own racing heartbeat filled her ears now, each breath faster and faster, filling her lungs with the scent of hay and leather.

Trailing her hand along the plush velvet of the horse's coat, she angled her way out of the wooden stall and into the walkway. "Hello, Mrs. McNair—" she swallowed hard "—and Stone."

Mariah McNair smiled. Stone didn't. In fact, he was scowling. But there was also something more lurking in his eyes, something…sad? She hated the way her heart pinched instinctively, and hated even more that she could still read him so well.

Mariah held out a hand. "Dear, let's step back into the office where we can chat in private."

With Stone, too? But Mariah's words weren't a question. "Of course."

Questions welled inside her with each step toward the office, passing Hidden Gem staff barely hiding their own curiosity as they prepped rides for vacationers. Alex and Amie eyed them but kept their distance as they hauled the saddles off their horses. The twins wore the same somber and stunned expressions on their faces that she saw on Stone's.

Concern nipped like a feisty foal, and Johanna walked faster. She'd all but grown up here, following her stable hand dad around. Her family hadn't been wealthy like the McNairs, but she'd always been loved, secure—until the day her family had died when their malfunctioning furnace caught on fire in the night.

She'd lost everything. Except rather than making her afraid to love, she craved that sense of family. These walls echoed with memories of how special those bonds had been.

Custom saddles lined the corridors, all works of art like everything the McNairs made. Carvings marked the leather with a variety of designs from roses to vines to full-out pastoral scenes. Some saddles sported silver or brass studs on horn caps and skirting edges that rivaled the tooling of any of the best old vaqueros.

Her job here had spoiled her for any other place. She couldn't imagine living anywhere else. This was her home as well as her workplace.

Stone held open the office door, which left her no choice but to walk past him, closely. His radiant heat brought back memories of his bare skin slick with perspiration against hers as they made love in the woods on a hot summer day.

His gaze held hers for an electrified moment, attraction crackling, alive and well, between them, before she forced herself to walk forward and break the connection.

Red leather chairs, a sofa and a heavy oak desk filled the paneled room. The walls were covered in framed prints of the McNair holdings at various stages of expansion. A portrait of Mariah and her husband, Jasper, on their twenty-fifth wedding anniversary dominated the space over a stone fireplace, a painting done shortly before Jasper had passed away from a heart attack.

Mariah's fingers traced lightly along the carved frame before she settled into a fat wingback chair with an exhausted sigh. "Please, have a seat, Johanna. Stone? Pour us something to drink, dear."

Johanna perched on the edge of a wooden rocker. "Mrs. McNair? Is there a problem?"

"I'm afraid there is, and I need your help."

"Whatever I can do, just let me know."

Mariah took a glass of sparkling spring water from her grandson, swallowed deeply, then set the crystal tumbler aside. "I'm having some health problems and during my treatment I need to be sure I have my life settled."

"Health problems?" Concern gripped Johanna's heart in a chilly fist. How much could she ask without being too pushy? Considering this woman had almost been her family, she decided she could press as far as she needed. "Is it serious?"

"Very," Mariah said simply, fingering her diamond horseshoe necklace. "I'm hopeful my doctors can buy me more time, but treatments will be consuming and I don't want the business or my pets to be neglected."

Mariah's love for her animals was one of the bonds the two women shared. The head of a billion-dollar empire had always made time for a stable hand's daughter who wanted to learn more about the animals at Hidden Gem.

Johanna took the glass from Stone, her hand shaking so much the ice rattled. "I'm sorry, more than I can say. What can I do to help?"

Angling forward, Mariah held her with clear blue eyes identical to Stone's. "You can help me find homes for my dogs."

Without hesitation, Johanna said, "I can watch them while you're undergoing treatments."

"My dear," Mariah said gently, but with a steely strength, "it's brain cancer. I believe it's best for my dogs to find permanent homes."

The pronouncement slammed Johanna back in her chair. She bit her bottom lip to hold in a gasp and blinked back tears. There were no words.

A firm hand landed on her shoulder. Stone's hand. She didn't have to look. She would know his touch anywhere.

God, he must be devastated. She angled around to clasp his hand, but the cool look in his eyes stopped her. Apparently, he was fine with giving out sympathy, but his pride wouldn't allow him to accept any from her.

Johanna reached to take Mariah's hands instead, holding them in hers. "I'll do whatever you need."

"Thank you." Mariah smiled and squeezed Johanna's hands. "Stone will be finding homes for my dogs, but I need for you to go with him and make sure the matches are truly right for each one. It should take about a week."

"A week?" she squeaked.

Go off alone with Stone for a week? No, no and hell, no. The torture of running across him here was bad enough, but at least they had the buffer of work. Stone had stolen her heart then trounced all her dreams of having a family of her own. He'd refused to consider having children or adopting. They'd argued—more than once—until finally she'd broken things off. He'd thought she was bluffing.

He was wrong.

Did Mariah think she was bluffing, as well?

Johanna chose her words carefully. "I don't mean any disrespect, ma'am, and I understand your need for peace, especially now…" She pushed back a well of emotion. This wasn't about her. It was about Mariah, and yes, Stone, too. "You have to realize this attempt at matchmaking isn't going to work. Stone and I were finished a long time ago."

Johanna shot a pointed look at him in case he might be harboring any thoughts of using this situation to wrangle his way back into her bed. Even when she'd broken things off, he'd been persistent for a solid month before accepting that she wouldn't change her mind.

He simply arched an arrogant eyebrow before shifting his glacial gaze toward his grandmother. Only then did his eyes warm.

Mariah shook her head. "I'm not trying anything of the sort. I have trusted you with my animals for years. I've watched you grow up, known you since you were in elementary school. You also understand Stone. He won't pull off anything questionable with you watching him. Can you think of anyone else he can't charm?"

Johanna conceded, "You have a point there."

Stone frowned, speaking for the first time, "Hey, I think I'm being insulted."

Mariah reached up to pat his cheek. "If you only *think* it, Stone, then I must not be making myself clear enough. I hope you will be successful in proving yourself, but I have serious reservations."

He scratched along his jaw, which was perpetually peppered with beard stubble no matter how often he shaved. "You trust Johanna over your own flesh and blood?"

"I do," Mariah said without hesitation. "Case in point, you wanted to keep the expansion a secret, even from me."

"Just until I had the details hammered out, to surprise you. To impress you."

"Our company isn't a grade-school art project to tape to the refrigerator. You need to show me you understand the importance of teamwork and compassion. That's the reason I came up with this test." Mariah's calm but unwavering tone made it clear there would be no changing her mind. "Johanna, you'll go with him to all the interviews with prospective families that I've lined up."

"You've already found the families? You're making his test too easy," Johanna said suspiciously. "There must be a catch."

"No catch. But as for easy?" Mariah laughed softly. "That depends on you two and your ability to act like grownups around each other."

"Civility during a few interviews," Johanna echoed. "We can handle that." Maybe.

"More than during interviews. There's travel time, as well."

"Travel?" So there was a catch. She glanced at Stone who was looking too damn hot—and smug—leaning against the fireplace mantel. He simply shrugged, staying tall, dark and silent.

"These families I've lined up don't live around the corner, but the corporate jet should make the journey easier." Mariah patted her diamond horseshoe necklace. "You should be able to complete the meet and greets in a week."

Stone stepped forward. "Gran, I can handle our travel arrangements."

"You can. But you're not going to. I'm calling the shots on this. My plan. My test," his grandmother said succinctly.

Stone's jaw clamped shut, and Johanna could see the lord of the boardroom holding himself back because of his grandmother's condition.

"A week…" Johanna repeated. A week away from work, a week of more than just crossing paths for a few meet and greets. "Alone together, jetting around the country on the McNair corporate airplane?"

"I don't expect the two of you to reunite. This truly is about Stone showing me he's capable of the compassion needed to run a company." Her hand slid up behind her neck and she unclasped the chain. "But I do hope the two of you can also find some way to reconcile your way back to friendship."

Understanding settled over Johanna. "You want to be at peace—knowing your dogs are loved *and* that Stone and I won't hurt each other again."

Mariah's fingers closed around her necklace and

whispered, "My grandson's well-being is important, more so than any company."

Mariah had found Johanna's Achilles' heel. Was it an act from Mariah, to get her way? Heaven knew the woman could be every bit as wily as Stone. But given Mariah's illness, the woman did deserve peace in every realm of her life.

"Okay," Johanna agreed simply.

Mariah pressed the necklace into Johanna's palm. "Good luck, dear."

Johanna started to protest such an extravagant gift, but one look in Mariah's eyes showed her how much it meant to her…a woman at the end of her life passing along pieces of herself. The horseshoe was so much more than diamonds. It was a gift of the heart, of family, a symbol of all Johanna wanted for her life.

All that Stone had thrown away without a thought.

She pitied him almost as much as she resented him for costing them the life they could have had together.

Her fist closed around the necklace, and she stood, facing Stone with a steely resolve she'd learned from Mariah. "Pack your bags, Casanova. We have a plane to catch."

Two

Staring out the office window, Stone listened for the door to click closed as his grandmother and Johanna left, then he sank into the leather desk chair, his shoulders hunched. He couldn't believe Johanna had actually agreed to a week alone on the road with him.

Heaven or hell?

He'd started to argue with Mariah, but she'd cut out on the conversation, claiming exhaustion. How could he dispute that? If anything, he wanted to wrap her in cotton to protect her even as she made her way to her favorite chaise longue chair up in her sitting room.

The prideful air that had shone in Mariah's eyes kept him from following her. Not to mention the intuitive sense that she needed to be alone. He understood the feeling, especially right now. He and his grandmother were alike in that, needing privacy and space to lick wounds. A hard sigh racked his body as he tamped down the urge to tear apart the whole office space—books, computers, saddles and framed awards—to rage at a world that would take away his grandmother.

The last thing he wanted to do was leave Fort Worth now and waste even one of her remaining days flying around the country. Even with Johanna.

What exactly was Mariah's angle in pairing them up on this Mutt Mission of Mercy? Was she making him jump through hoops like one of her trained dogs to see how badly he wanted to run the company, to prove he had a heart? Or was she matchmaking, as Johanna had accused? If so, this wasn't about the company at all, which should reassure him.

More likely his multitasking, masterminding grandmother was looking to kill two birds with one stone—matchmaking and putting him through the wringer to make him appreciate what he'd inherit when he took the reins of the company.

He just had to get through the next seven days with his former fiancée without rehashing the train wreck of their messy breakup where she'd pointed out all his emotional shortcomings. He couldn't give Johanna what she'd wanted from him—a white picket fence family life. He wasn't wired that way. He truly was aptly named. He might have overcome the rough start in life, born with an addiction, spending most of his first ten years catching up on developmental delays—but some betrayals left scars so thick and deep he might as well be made of stone.

He understood full well his grandmother's concerns about him were true, even if he disagreed about the company needing a soft-hearted marshmallow at the helm. Although God knew he would do anything to give his grandmother peace, whatever her motivation for this doggy assignment. The business was all he would have left of her and he didn't intend to throw that away because hanging out with Johanna opened him up to a second round of falling short. His hand fisted on the chair's armrests as he stared out at the rolling fields filled with vacationers riding into the woods.

No, he didn't expect a magical fix-it with the only woman he'd ever considered marrying. But he needed closure. Because he couldn't stop thinking about her. And he was growing weary of her avoiding him.

Truth be told, he would give his right arm for the chance to sleep with Johanna again. And again. And most certainly again, because she ruled his thoughts until he hadn't been able to touch another woman since their breakup seven months ago. That was a damn long time to go without.

The life of a monk didn't suit him. Frustration pumped through him, making him ache to punch a wall. He dragged in breaths of air and forced his fists to unfurl along the arms of the chair.

A hand rested lightly on his shoulder.

Stone jolted and pivoted around fast. "Johanna? You've been there the whole time?"

He'd assumed she'd left with his grandmother.

"I started to tell you, but you seemed…lost in thought. I was searching for the right moment to clear my throat or something, and that moment just never came."

She'd stood there the whole time, watching him struggle to hold in his grief over his grandmother's announcement? The roomy office suddenly felt smaller now that he was alone with Johanna. The airplane would be damn near claustrophobic as they jetted across the country with his grandmother's pack of dogs.

"What did you need?" His voice came out chilly even to his own ears, but he had a tight rein on his emotions right now.

Johanna pulled her hand off his shoulder awkwardly. "Are you okay?"

There was a time when they hadn't hesitated to put their hands all over each other. That time had passed. A wall stood between them now, and he had no one to blame but himself. "What do you mean?"

Her sun-kissed face flooded with compassion. "Your grandmother just told you she has terminal cancer. That has to be upsetting."

"Of course it is. To you, too, I imagine." The wall between him and Johanna kept him from reaching out to comfort her.

"I'm so sorry." She twisted her fingers in front of her, the chain from the diamond horseshoe necklace dangling. "You have to know that regardless of what happened between us, I do still care about your family…and you."

She *cared* about him?

What a wishy-washy word. *Cared.* What he felt for her was fiery, intense and, yes, even at times filled with frustrated anger that they couldn't be together, and he couldn't forget about her when they were apart. "You *care* about my family, and that's why you agreed to my grandmother's crazy plan." It wasn't that she wanted to be alone with him.

"It influenced my decision, yes." She shuffled from dusty boot to dusty boot, drawing his attention to her long legs. "I also care about her dogs and I respect that she wants to look after their welfare. She's an amazing woman."

"Yes, she is." An enormity of emotion about his grandmother's health problems welled inside him, pain and anger combatting for dominance, both due to the grinding agony that he couldn't fix this. Feeling powerless went against everything in his nature.

It made him rage inside all over again, and only exacerbated the frustration over months of rejection from Johanna.

Over months of missing her.

Something grouchy within him made him do the very thing guaranteed to push Johanna away. Although arguing with her felt better than being ignored.

He stepped closer, near enough to catch a whiff of hay and bluebonnets, and closed his hands over her fingers, which were gripping the necklace his grandmother had given her. Johanna's eyes went wide, but she didn't move away, so he pressed ahead.

Dipping his head, Stone whispered against the curve of her neck, "Do you feel sorry enough for me to do anything about it?"

She flattened a hand on his chest, finally stopping him short. But her breathing was far from steady and she still hadn't pushed him away.

"Not *anything*." Her eyes narrowed, and he knew he'd pushed her far enough for now.

He backed away and hitched a hip on the heavy oak desk he'd climbed over as a kid. His initials were still carved underneath. "You've come back to offer comfort. Mission complete. Thanks."

"You're not fooling me." Her emerald-green eyes went from angry to sad in a revealing instant. "I know you better than anyone."

He reached for her fist, which was still holding the necklace from his grandmother, and drew Johanna toward him until her hand rested against his heart. "Then tell me what I'm feeling right now."

"You're trying to get me to run by making a move on me, because I'm touching a nerve with questions about your grandmother," she said with unerring accuracy. He never had been able to get anything past her. "You're in pain and you don't want me to see that."

"I'm in pain, all right—" his eyes slid down the fine length of her curvy, toned body "—and I'm more than happy to let you see everything."

She tugged away from him, shaking her head. "For a practiced, world-class charmer, you're overplaying your hand."

"But you're not unaffected." He slipped the necklace from her fist deftly.

Standing, he put the chain around her neck as if that had been his reason for coming closer. He brushed aside the tail of her thick braid. Her chest rose and fell faster. As he worked the clasp, he savored the satiny skin of her neck, then skimmed his fingers forward along the silvery links, settling the diamond horseshoe between her breasts. Her heartbeat fluttered against his knuckles.

"Stone, our attraction to each other was never in question," she said bluntly, her hands clenched at her sides and her chin tipping defiantly. "Because of that attraction, we need to have ground rules for this trip."

"Ground rules?"

She met his gaze full-on. "No more of these seduction games. If you want *me* to play nice, then *you* be nice."

"Define *nice*." He couldn't resist teasing.

"Being truthful, polite—" Her eyes glinted like emeralds. "And above all, no games."

"I thought your only agenda here was making sure the dogs end up in good homes." He toyed with the diamond horseshoe, barely touching her. A little taste of Johanna went a long way.

"I can place the dogs without you," she said confidently. "I'm agreeing to your grandmother's plan to give her peace of mind on a broader spectrum. She wants us to make this trip together, and the only way I can manage that is if you stop with the practiced seduction moves. Be real. Be honest."

"Fine then." He slid the horseshoe back and forth along the chain, just over her skin, like a phantom touch. "In all honesty, I can assure you that I ache to peel off your clothes with my teeth. I burn to kiss every inch of your bared skin. And my body burns to make love to you again and again, because, hell, yes, I want to forget about what my grandmother just told me."

He dropped the charm and waited.

She exhaled long and hard, her eyes wide. "Okay, then. I hear you, and I believe you."

Shoving away from the desk and around her, he strutted right to the door and stopped short, waiting until she turned to look at him.

"Oh, Johanna, one last thing." He met her gaze dead-on, her eyes as appealing as her curves. "I wanted you every bit as much before my grandmother's announcement. This has nothing to do with me needing consolation. See you in the morning, sunshine."

Johanna had until morning to pack her bags and get her hormones under control.

Moonlight cast a dappled path through the pine trees as she walked the gravel lane from the barn to her cabin. Her heart ached as much as her muscles after this long day. Too long.

She opened her mailbox and tugged out a handful of flyers and a pizza coupon. Laughter from vacationers rode the wind as they enjoyed a party on the back deck of the main lodge, the splash of the hot tub mingling with the trickling echo of the creek that ran behind her little hideaway house.

Since graduation from vet tech school four years ago, she'd lived in a two-bedroom cabin on the Hidden Gem Ranch, the same cabin model used by vacationers. She liked to think of it as home, but truth be told she hadn't had a home since her parents' trailer had burned down when she was eighteen. She'd lived in an apartment during her two years of vet tech training, thanks to a scholarship from Mariah McNair. Then Johanna had accepted a job at Hidden Gem after graduation, her girlhood crush on Stone flourishing into full-out love.

Day by day, she'd earned a living, marking time, doing a job she adored but never putting down roots of her own, waiting on Prince Charming to pop the question. Once he did, she discovered her prince was a frog. A hot, sexy frog. But a frog nonetheless. She couldn't blame Stone for how things shook down between them. She was the one who'd worn blinders, refusing to accept the truth until it was too late.

But with the silver chain around her neck, the diamond horseshoe cool against her skin, she could only feel the weight of impending loss, the finality of closing the book on this chapter of her life. Once Mariah died, there would be nothing left holding Johanna here. Nothing other than her tenacious attraction to Stone, but that only kept her from moving on with another man, finding a future for herself with the family she craved.

She pushed open the gate on her split rail fence. The

night air carried the refrain of square-dancing music from the sound system that fed the pool area. Maybe she needed this trip away from the ranch for more reasons than she'd thought. Perhaps this wasn't just about finding peace for Mariah, but snipping the last bonds that held her to Stone so she could move on without regrets.

She climbed the three wooden steps up to her dark log cabin, katydids buzzing a full-out Texas symphony. A creak just ahead stopped her in her tracks. She searched the railed porch, wishing she'd remembered to leave on a front light, but she hadn't expected to come home so late. She blinked her eyes fast to better adjust to the dark and found a surprise waiting for her in one of the two rocking chairs.

Amie McNair sat with a gray tabby cat in her lap, a Siamese at her feet, both hers, soon to have feline siblings when Mariah's pride joined them.

"Well, hey, there," Amie drawled. "I didn't think you would ever get home."

What was Amie's reason for waiting around? Was she here to talk about Mariah's announcement? The impending loss had to be hard on the whole family. She and Amie weren't enemies but they weren't BFFs, either. They were more like childhood acquaintances who had almost been related. And because of that connection, she felt the need to hug this woman on what had to be one of the most difficult days of her life.

Johanna unlocked the front door and reached inside to turn on the porch light. "I worked late preparing to leave tomorrow, but I'm here now." She let the screen door close again. "Is there something I can do for you?"

"Ah, so you're actually going through with my grandmother's plan." Amie swept her hand over the tabby, sending a hint of kitty dander wafting into the night air as her bracelets jingled.

Even covered in cat hair and a light sheen of perspiration, Amie was a stunner, totally gorgeous no matter what she wore. She'd been the first runner-up in the Miss Texas pageant ten years ago, reportedly the first beauty competition she'd lost since her mother had teased up her hair and sent Amie tap-dancing out on the stage at four years old. She'd tap-danced her way through puberty into bikinis and spray tans. Johanna remembered well how Amie's mama had lived for her daughter's wins.

Johanna settled into the cedar rocker beside Amie and the cats, reluctant to go into her cabin. Inside, she had nothing to do but pace around, unable to sleep because of this crazy, upside down day. "I don't have a choice but to go with Stone and the dogs."

"Sure you do." Amie kicked off her sandals and stroked her toes over the kitty at her feet. "Tell my grandmother no, that it's not fair to play with your life this way. You know as well as I do that you can find homes for those dogs all on your own."

"True enough, and of course I've thought of that. Except any…unease…I feel doesn't matter, not in light of what's important to Mariah. She's dying, Amie." The reality of those words still stole her breath for a long, humid moment. "How can I deny her anything, even if the request is bizarre?"

Amie blinked back tears and looked away, her sleek black ponytail trailing over one shoulder. "I refuse to accept she's going to die. The doctors will buy her enough time so she can pass away at a ripe old age." Her throat moved with a long swallow before she looked at Johanna again, her eyes cleared of grief. "Mariah can be reasoned with…unless you don't really want to say no."

An ugly suspicion bloomed in Johanna's mind. "Or is it you who wants me to walk away so your cousin loses?"

Amie's perfectly plucked eyebrows arched upward. "That wouldn't be very loyal of me."

"Yet you're not denying anything. What's really going on?" She hated to think Amie could be so coldly calculating, but then she'd always had the sense the woman wanted more power in the family business.

The former beauty queen spread her hands. Long fingers that had once played the piano to accompany her singing now crafted high-end jewelry. "I've never made a secret of the fact that I want my family to take me seriously." Her hair swished over her shoulder, the porch light catching on the gems in the Aztec design of her hair clamp. "I'm just weighing in with my thoughts on this whole 'test' game. This is not the way to decide the future of our family legacy."

"What's *your* test?"

"Gran hasn't told me yet. Or Alex, either, for that matter." Amie scrunched her nose. In frustration? Or at the smoky scent of a bonfire launching an acrid tint to the night breeze? "But after what she set up for Stone, I'm not hopeful mine will make sense. I'm just trying to protect us all."

Johanna thumbed a knotty circle on the armrest. "How is talking to me going to accomplish that?"

"You're the only one who has ever come close to getting through the walls Stone puts around himself. I just hope you'll make sure he's okay."

Johanna sat up straighter. "Excuse me?"

"Be sure he doesn't crack up over this."

"Crack up? Stone? He's rock-solid—no pun intended."

Amie clamped Johanna's arm in a surprisingly strong grip. "I'm worried about him, okay? He doesn't have a support system like I do. My brother and I can tell each other everything. Stone is our family, but he's never let himself get close to us. And I'm worried about him right now."

There was no denying the sincerity in her voice.

"That's really sweet of you." Johanna felt bad for assuming the worst. "I do care about Stone, even though we can't be together. He's a strong man. He will grieve for Mariah—we all will—but he will haul himself through. He always does."

Even as she said it, she couldn't ignore a niggling voice in the back of her mind reminding her that Stone's childhood had been very different from her own or that of his twin cousins. His grandmother had been his only bedrock of support.

Amie's hand slid away. "Just keep what I said in mind. That's all I ask." Cradling her cat in her arms, she stood. "Good night and good luck with your trip."

"Thank you…" She had a feeling she would need luck and more to get through the coming week. She needed a plan and stronger boundaries to protect her heart.

"Anytime," Amie called over her shoulder as strolled down the steps as though she were taking a runway scene by storm, leaving her shoes behind, her other cat following her into the night.

Scooping up her junk mail, Johanna shoved to her feet. She needed to start packing now if she wanted any chance of getting to bed at a reasonable time. Not that she expected to sleep much with her brain whirling a million miles an hour.

She'd tried to make this place her own, with everything from sunflowers in the front yard to a quilted wreath on the door. Hokey? Maybe. But she'd dreamed of hokey and normal as a kid listening to the rain rattling along the tin roof of their trailer.

She pushed her way inside. The scent of freshly waxed floors and flowers greeted her, but not even a cat or dog of her own. So many times she'd wondered why she never chose a pet for herself, just took care of other people's....

Wait.

Her nose twitched.

Waxed floors and...flowers? She didn't have any inside, not even a floral air freshener.

Patting along the wall, she found the switch and flipped on the light. A wagon wheel chandelier splashed illumination around the room full of fat stuffed furniture in paisley patterns, a girly escape for a tomboy in a dusty, mucky profession. She spun to scan the room, her eyes landing on her shabby chic sofa.

Where a man was sprawled out asleep.

Her gaze skated from the boots on the armrest, up muscular legs in jeans, past a Diamonds in the Rough belt buckle, to broad shoulders in a blue flannel shirt. For a second, she thought Stone had followed her here. A straw cowboy hat covered the man's face as he snored softly.

Although once she looked closer, she realized it wasn't Stone at all. It was his near twin. His cousin

Alex was asleep on her sofa, with a fistful of wild daisies on his chest.

As she saw him waiting there for her, she couldn't help but think, Amie and Alex didn't tell each other everything.

Three

Johanna swept the cowboy hat from Alex's face. "What are you doing in my house?"

He peeked out of one eye lazily, scrubbed a hand over his face and yawned. Stretching, he sat up, keeping his hold on the daisies, apparently in no hurry to answer her question.

Alex rarely rushed. Yet he always seemed to get crazy amounts done. He was a fascinating individual, like all the McNairs. And while he'd been in her cabin often, she hadn't expected to see him here tonight.

"Well?" She hitched her hands on her hips. "Do you have anything to say for yourself? I locked the door, so you're breaking and entering."

"As your *landlord*," he drawled, his voice like Southern Comfort on the rocks, smooth with a bite. Stone spoke in more clipped, bass tones—like boulders rumbling. "I used my master key. I own the place."

She'd known Alex as long as she'd known Stone. She'd met all of the McNairs when her father took a stable hand job here during Johanna's third-grade year. Where Stone was the outgoing, bad-boy charmer, Alex had been the brooding, silent type, a tenacious rodeo champ even as a kid, breaking more bones by eighteen than any pro football star.

After she'd ended her engagement to Stone, she'd realized Alex's resolute nature had hidden a longtime attraction to her. Six months after the split, Alex had made his move by asking her out to dinner. She'd been stunned—and not ready to consider dating anyone. He'd taken the news well. Or so she'd thought. She was beginning to grasp how persistent, patient and downright stubborn this quiet giant could be.

With that in mind, she should have realized their grandmother's plan would not go over well with Alex. "Even though you own my rental cabin, I didn't realize landlords slept on the sofa," she joked, needing to keep things light. Her emotional well was running on empty. "Do you have a specific reason for being here?"

"I'm making sure you don't fall under my evil cousin's spell again." He swung his legs to the floor and thrust out the fistful of daisies.

Roots straggled from a couple of the stems. He definitely was a unique one with a charm all his own. At another time in her life she might have been tempted.

She took the daisies from him. "You're trying to persuade me by giving me flowers?"

"Consider it elaborate bribery," he said with a self-deprecating grin directed at the raggedy bouquet.

"You stole them out of the garden by the back deck," she shot over her shoulder as she stepped into the kitchen area to get a large mason jar.

"The garden belongs to me."

"To your family." She slid the flowers into the jar and tucked it under the faucet.

"Same thing." His smile faded. "Are you okay with this trip?"

"Your concern is sweet and I do mean that." She smiled, then jerked as water overflowed from the jar and splashed onto her hand.

"My motives are purer than Amie's were out there on the porch."

"You heard her?"

"I did, since you always leave your windows open rather than use the air conditioner." He stretched his legs out in front of him, crossing his boots at the ankles as he extended his arms along the back of the couch. "You would be wise to remember she's the most ruthless of all of us."

"That's not a very nice thing to say." She placed the flowers on the end table by the floral sofa, a perfect match for the rustic charm of her place.

"I only mean that you're my friend." He reached for her hand and tugged her down to sit beside him. "You and Amie don't have that kind of relationship. She's thinking of the family. I'm worried about you."

Johanna looked into his eyes, the same unique shade of light blue as Stone's. Though born three years apart, the men could have been twins. Alex was actually better suited for her. They had more in common. Alex ran a family ranch, whereas Stone was the king of the boardroom, such a workaholic he'd made it clear he had little room in his life for white-picket dreams.

Yet, as she sat here inches away from this incredibly sexy cowboy who'd just given her the sweetest flowers, she could only think of how much she'd wanted Stone to kiss her earlier. And Alex left her lukewarm, and it wasn't fair to keep stringing him along.

She touched his wrist. "Alex, we need to talk about—"

The front door opened with a knock in progress, no real warning at all. Johanna jolted, nearly falling off the sofa as she turned to face the intruder.

Stone stood in the open door, scowling, holding a handful of purple tulips.

What the hell?

Standing in Johanna's doorway, Stone cricked his neck from side to side, trying to process what his eyes told him. His cousin Alex sat on the sofa with Johanna. Close to Johanna. So near, their thighs pressed against each other and before she'd jolted away, she'd been leaning in, her hand on Alex's arm.

And there were fresh flowers on the end table.

Stone strode inside and tossed the tulips—ones that he'd pulled out of a vase in the lobby of the main lodge—onto the end table beside the daisies that looked remarkably like ones in the garden by the deck.

"Sorry to have interrupted…" Whatever had been about to happen. His pulse hammered behind his eyes; his head pounded in frustration over a hellish day that was spiraling down the drain faster and faster by the second.

Nibbling her bottom lip, Johanna rubbed her palms along her jeans. "At the risk of sounding cliché, this isn't what it looks like."

"What does it look like?" Stone smiled, somehow managing to keep his tone level in spite of the jealousy pumping through him.

"That Alex and I are a couple. We're not." She glanced at Alex apologetically.

That apologetic look spoke volumes. His cousin had

been trying to make a move on her. His cousin—as close as any brother—had fallen for Johanna. The thought stunned and rattled Stone into silence.

Alex stood, a gleam in his eyes just like when he'd reached the boiling point as a kid—just before he decked whoever had pissed him off. He leveled that gaze at Stone and slung an arm around Johanna's shoulders. "Who says we're not a couple?"

She shrugged off his arm. "Stop riling him up on purpose. You two are not teenagers anymore." She jabbed a finger at Stone. "That goes for you, too. No fights."

"I'm just looking for a straight answer." Stone spread his arms.

Johanna went prickly. "What this is or isn't doesn't concern you."

"Sure it does," he said, his tone half-joking, but his intent dead serious. "If you've been seeing each other and didn't bother to tell me, that's damn inconsiderate of my feelings."

Alex snorted. "Your *feelings?* You're joking, right?"

Stone resisted the urge to punch Alex in the face and forced reason through the fog. "You're yanking my chain on purpose. Why?"

"Just making a point. Johanna is important to this family and not just because she was your fiancée. If you hurt her," Alex said softly, lethally, "I'll kick your ass."

Fair enough.

They had the same goal: protecting her. Stone respected that. He nodded curtly. "Message heard and received."

Johanna whistled sharply between her teeth, like when she called a horse. "Hey, boys? Don't I get any say here?"

Stone shifted his focus from Alex to her. "Of course. What would you like to add?"

She rolled her eyes. "Nothing. Absolutely nothing. I'm completely capable of taking care of myself. Thank you both for your concern, but I need to pack for this trip tomorrow."

"Of course you can look after yourself," Stone said, gesturing for Alex to go out the door ahead of him. Then he took that moment's privacy to lean toward Johanna. "Just wanted to bring the tulips and say thank-you for caring about my grandmother's happiness."

She went still, most likely in shock, her hand drifting down to rest on top of the purple tulips. He used her moment of distraction to kiss her, just once, on the mouth, but good God, even a brief taste of Johanna was more potent than…anything. After seven months without the feel of her, his body shouted for more.

For everything.

Desire cracked like a whip inside him. He pulled back before he lost control and pushed his luck too far. "See you in the morning at the landing strip."

He closed the door behind him, the night sounds of bugs and owls, the wind in the trees, wrapping around him. He sucked in two deep breaths to steady himself before facing his cousin again.

Alex leaned against the porch post, tucking his hat on his head. "I meant what I said in there about kicking your ass."

"How serious is it? Whatever the two of you have going on?" What the hell would he do if his cousin was all-in? Or worse yet, if Johanna harbored feelings, too?

"If you care so much who she's seeing," Alex said ambiguously, "then do something about it." Without another word, he shoved away from the post, jogged down the steps and disappeared into the dark.

Stone stood on the porch, the smell of the tulips and the feel of Johanna still fresh in his senses even though he'd left her and the flowers inside. But then she'd been in his thoughts every damn second since their split.

His cousin was right. Stone was still attracted to Johanna, and it was time to do something about it.

Stone's kiss still tinged her lips and her memory.

Johanna hauled her suitcase out from under the bed and tossed it onto the mattress with a resounding thump. What the hell had he been thinking, kissing her like that? Although he hadn't lingered. Some might call it a friendly kiss. Except they had this history together….

Need coursed through her, hot and molten, with just a splash of sweetness, like the scent of the tulips she'd brought with her into the bedroom. They rested under the lamp, purple splashes of color on the white table.

She'd tried her best to tamp down her attraction to Stone these past months, which was easier to do when their paths rarely crossed. How would she survive a week of time alone with him?

She dropped to sit on the edge of her bed, the white iron headboard tapping the wall. She tugged one of the purple tulips from the bunch and skimmed it against her mouth lightly. She knew he'd certainly stolen them from a vase in the lodge, and she couldn't help but note how both cousins had snagged the closest flowers at hand. They could drape women in jewels from their family business, yet they still understood the value of a well-timed bouquet.

Stone's tulips, and his kiss, were picking away at her

defenses. Too bad she couldn't wedge a coat of armor into her suitcase to withstand the barrage on her hormones.

Laughter with a hysterical edge bubbled out of her, and she flopped back on the bed into the cushiony softness of her pink-and-gray chevron quilt. She clasped the tulip against her chest, watching the ceiling fan click lazy circles above her. She and Stone had spent entire weekends in her bed making love. She hadn't wanted to go to his quarters in the main house, not even after they'd gotten engaged, not with his grandmother in a nearby suite. So he'd taken her on elaborate trips, vowing that he did so because then he could at least feel like she was staying with him.

Now Johanna wondered if she'd known they were destined to fail even from the start. Their time together had been a fantasy that couldn't withstand the light of harsh reality.

She hadn't traveled much before Stone. During her year dating Stone, he'd flown her to exotic locales and swanky fund-raisers held by influential billionaires, a world away from her ranch and Stetson day-to-day life.

What should she expect from this trip?

She rolled to her side and stared into the empty suitcase. What did a girl take to a week of doggie dates with mystery families and her ex-fiancé? More importantly, how would she react if he gave her another one of those impromptu kisses?

A tap on the window snapped her out of her daze.

She jolted upright, her heart pounding in alarm. Before she could even reach for the cell phone her eyes focused on the face in the glass pane.

Stone stood outside like a Lone Star Romeo.

Her pulse leaped. Damn her traitorous body.

She rolled from the bed and to her feet. She shoved the window up, the muggy night breeze rolling inside and fluttering the lace curtains. "What are you doing out there?"

"I forgot my flowers. You didn't seem to want them, so I figured I would give them to someone who would appreciate them." He hefted himself up and through the window before she could blink.

She stumbled back a step, watching him eye her room, walk to the flowers then peer out the door.

Realization dawned, along with a spark of anger. "You're checking to make sure your cousin didn't come back here."

"Maybe I am." He turned on his heels to face her again. His gaze fell to her bed, right where the lone tulip lay.

Feeling vulnerable, she rushed to scoop up the flower and said, "I'm trying to decide what to pack for the trip. Since I don't know where we're going, I'm not making much progress."

"Pack comfortably." The gleam in his eyes projected loud and clear that he wasn't fooled. "If we need something more, I'll buy it for you."

"We're not engaged anymore. You're not buying me clothes or other gifts." She'd returned all the jewelry after she'd broken up with him—everything, including a yellow diamond engagement ring with a double halo setting. The night he'd given it to her, she'd thought all of her dreams of a family and a real home had come true.

She'd grown up a lot in the past seven months, alone with her disillusionment.

"Johanna," he drawled, "we may not be engaged, but you are an employee of Hidden Gem Ranch and if you're on Hidden Gem business and need clothes, the company can pick up the bill."

"Clothes for what, exactly?"

"There's a gem trade show I want to catch while we're out."

She knew how elaborate and hoity-toity those events could get. Being with him at one of those shows would feel too much like a fancy date. "I'll stay at the hotel with the dogs."

"We'll see," he said in that stubborn, noncommittal way of his just before he swung a leg out the window again. "Good night."

"Stone?"

He stopped shy of stepping all the way through the window. "Yes?"

"Thanks for the flowers." She strode closer—just to be ready to close the window when he left, not to be nearer to him. Right? "It really is sweet how much you care about your grandmother's happiness. I always admired that about you, your family loyalty."

"Glad you have good memories, not just bad."

Guilt pinched her over how their breakup had hurt him, too. She touched his shoulder lightly. "There's nothing between Alex and me."

"I'm glad to hear that."

Was it her imagination or had he swayed closer?

She pressed a hand to his chest. "That doesn't mean there will never be someone. Am I not allowed to have another relationship again?"

A smile played with his mouth. "I'm not answering that."

He looked over his shoulder at the yard.

She frowned. "Is something wrong?"

"Uh, actually—" he glanced back at her sheepishly "—I was taking the dogs for a run. Hope you don't mind they're digging up your yard right now."

She laughed, enjoying this Stone, more like the man she remembered falling for, playful and open. "We're just lucky they didn't jump my little split rail fence."

"Since they're going to be spending the next week with me flying around in a plane, it would be a good idea to remind them who I am."

She allowed herself to fall just a little more under his spell again, even if only for a minute. "That's very sweet of you."

"Sweet? First you make out with my cousin and then you call me sweet. Twice." He shook his head, tsking. "This is not my night."

Before she could help herself, she blurted out, "I wasn't kissing your cousin."

"Good." Stone cupped the back of her neck and drew her in for a kiss, the full-out kind that proved to be a lot more than mouth meeting mouth.

His body pressed to hers in a familiar wall of muscle. Her lips parted and heaven help her, she didn't regret it. She sank into the sensation of having his hands on her again, the warmth of his tongue boldly meeting hers. Kisses like this could lure her into forgetting a lot. In their time apart, somehow she'd lost sight of how intensely their physical attraction could sweep away reason.

Heat gathered between her legs until she gripped his arms, her fingers digging deep. A husky moan of pleasure and need welled up in her throat. She was so close to losing control altogether, what with a bed only a few short steps away. They may have had so many issues in their relationship, but when it came to sex, they were in perfect synchronicity.

How was she going to walk away from him after a kiss like this?

The ground tipped under her feet…or wait…Stone was stumbling into her. She braced a hand on her dresser for balance and realized Ruby the Rottweiler had both paws on the open window and she was nudging Stone in the back. Gem the yellow lab sprung up to join the Rottie, a symphony of barking echoing from beneath them. A quick glance down confirmed that Pearl the terrier and Sterling the Chihuahua-dachshund mix danced in the bushes below.

Breathlessly, she whispered, "I think it's time for you to go."

"Sleep well, beautiful." Stone winked once before sliding back out the window.

She should have slammed the window closed after him. Instead, she stood between the parted curtains and watched him gather the pack with ease. He guided the larger dogs to jump her fence while scooping up the two little ones.

No question, she was in serious trouble here with only one way to cope during the coming week. She had to make absolutely sure she and Stone did not touch each other, not even accidentally. First thing in the morning, she intended to make her hands-off edict clear. Her eyes clung to the breadth of his shoulders and lower to his perfect butt that rivaled any blue jeans ad ever.

Gritting her teeth, she slammed the window closed and spun away fast.

Damn, it was going to be a long, achy night.

* * *

The morning sun crept upward at the McNairs' private landing strip, which was located on the ranch. Johanna had given up waiting for Stone in the limousine an hour ago and had moved inside the small airport offices. The space held a waiting area, a control desk and a back room with a cot for a pilot to take naps if needed. There wasn't much else to do but sit. She could understand Stone being late to meet her, but his grandmother was here with her dogs, prolonging a farewell that already had to be horribly difficult.

Mariah held herself rigidly in control, Ruby and Gem each resting against one leg. Pearl and Sterling curled up together on a seat beside her. Johanna couldn't help but wonder how well the pack would adjust to being separated.

She checked the large digital clock above the door. The red numbers blinked nearly ten o'clock while the pilot kept busy with some paperwork outside beneath a Texas flag flapping lazily in the soft breeze. She bit back anger. She was exhausted from lack of sleep and frustrated from bracing herself to appear blasé in front of Stone.

Only to have him freakin' stand her up.

She was mad. Steaming mad. And completely confused. If he was playing mind games with her, that was one thing. But to involve his grandmother? That was plain wrong, and not like him.

Shuffling a seat to move closer to Mariah, Johanna put a reassuring hand on the woman's arm. "You don't have to do this, Mrs. McNair. The dogs can stay with you. They can stay here now and even if the time comes…" She swallowed back a lump of emotion. "Even if the time comes when you're not here. This is their home."

Mariah patted Johanna's hand. "It's okay, really. I love them enough to do what's best for them. I'll be in and out of the hospital quite often, and they deserve attention."

"Everyone here will take care of them." She held on tighter to this strong, brilliant woman who was already showing signs of fading away. She had new gaunt angles and a darkness around her eyes that showed her exhaustion in spite of keeping up appearances of normalcy with a red denim dress and boots. "You must realize that."

"I do, but I need to know they're settled permanently, for my own peace of mind." Mariah stroked the scruffy little terrier, adjusting the dog's bejeweled collar. "They deserve to be a part of a family and not just a task for the staff, or an obligation for a relative who doesn't really want them."

"They could be a comfort to you. Even if you kept one of them, like Pearl or Sterling, maybe…"

Mariah's touch skimmed from pup to pup until she'd petted all four. "I couldn't choose. It would be like playing favorites with my children or grandchildren."

There was an undeniable truth in her words and a selflessness that made Johanna ache all over again at the thought of losing her. "I wish there were more people like you in the world."

"You're dear to say that." She cradled Johanna's face in her hands. "And I wish you could be my granddaughter."

There it was. Out there. The unacknowledged big pink elephant that had sat in the middle of every one of their conversations for the past seven months. Mariah had never once interfered or questioned her decision to break it off with Stone.

If only there'd been some other way.

Johanna leaned in and hugged Mariah, whispering in her ear, "I'm so sorry I can't make that come true for you. I would have liked very much to have you as part of my family."

Mariah squeezed her once before easing away and thumbing a lone tear from the corner of her eye. "I just want you to be happy."

"My job makes me happy." True, but she'd once dreamed of much more. "If it weren't for your scholarship, I never could have afforded the training. I know I've thanked you before, but I can never thank you enough."

"Ah, dear." Mariah brushed back a loose strand from Johanna's braid. "This isn't goodbye. Even worst-case scenario, I'll be around for months, and you're only going to be gone a week. I intend to fight hard to be around as long as I can."

"I know." Johanna fidgeted with the horseshoe necklace. "I just want to be sure all the important things are said."

"Of course, but I don't want us to use our time on morbid thoughts or gloominess." Mariah smoothed her denim dress and sat straighter. "Stone in particular has had enough disappointment from the people he loves."

Johanna looked into the woman's deep blue eyes and read her in an instant. "You're sending him away this week so he won't be here as you start your treatments."

"Just until I get settled into a routine."

The closeness of the moment, the importance of this

time, emboldened her. "What if he wants to be around to support you?"

"My choices trump anyone else's right now," Mariah said with a steely strength that had made her a business-woman of national stature. "Keep Stone busy and take care of placing my dogs. Enjoy the time away from the ranch. You work too hard, and if I've learned anything lately, it's that we shouldn't waste a day."

Mariah eased the lecture with another squeeze of her hand, which Johanna quickly returned.

"Yes, ma'am."

"Good enough, and for goodness' sake, quit calling me Mrs. McNair or ma'am. If you can't call me Gran, then call me Mariah." She sighed, before shoving slowly to her feet. "Now how about we track down my tardy grandson so you can start your journey?"

"I'm sure he's on his way…Mariah." Johanna glanced at the wall clock again. This wasn't like him. Could something have happened?

Johanna's cell phone chimed from her purse, play-ing a vintage Willie Nelson love song. She glanced at Mariah, a blush stinging her cheeks faster than the fierce Texas sun. Damn it, why hadn't she changed her Stone ringtone? She should have swapped her ringtone to some broken heart, broken truck country song. There were sure plenty to pick from. She fished out her cell, fum-bling with the on button before putting it to her ear. "Where are you?"

"I'm at the office downtown." Stone's bass rumbled over her ears sending a fresh shiver of awareness down her spine. "A few unavoidable emergencies came up with work. I'll give you a call when I'm ready to leave."

Not a chance in hell was he getting off that easy, but

she didn't intend to chew him out with his grandmother listening. She would go straight to the Diamonds in the Rough headquarters and haul him out with both hands, if need be. Not that she intended to give him any warning. "Sure, thanks for calling."

She disconnected and turned to Mariah. "He's fine, just delayed downtown at the Fort Worth office. He wants me to swing by with the dogs, and we'll leave from there. Would you like to help me load the dogs in the car?"

"Of course." Mariah brightened at the task. "But please, take my limo. I'll have the airport security run me back to the house."

Johanna started to argue, but then the notion of rolling up to Diamonds in the Rough, Incorporated in the middle of downtown Fort Worth, dogs in tow, sounded like one hell of an entrance.

Her Texas temper fired up and ready, she was through letting Stone McNair walk all over her emotions.

Four

Stone hated like hell being late for anything, but crisis after crisis had cropped up at the office even though he'd come in at five in the morning to prep for his week-long departure.

Parked at his desk in front of the computer, he finished with the last details, clearing his calendar and rescheduling as much as he could for teleconferences from the road. He loved his grandmother, but she had to know the CEO of Diamonds in the Rough couldn't just check out for a week without major prep. That was the primary reason for her test, right? For him to prove he was best suited to run the company.

She couldn't have chosen a worse time.

Their CFO had gone into premature labor and had been placed on bed rest. His personal assistant was stuck in an airport in North Dakota. Their showroom was still under repairs from tornado damage and the construction crew's foreman had gone on strike.

And his grandmother was dying of cancer.

His hands clenched over the keyboard. For her, he'd put together detailed plans for taking Diamonds in the Rough to an international level, to expand the company as a tribute to his grandparents who'd been there for him over the years. Yet now she might not even live long enough to see that dream come to fruition. It cut him to the core to think he'd somehow let her down, but he must have since she felt she needed to concoct tests for him to prove himself.

His eyes slid to the wood drafting table littered with new designs, most of them done by Amie, but a few of his own were scattered through the mix. He sketched late at night, after hours, to ease the tension of the corporate rat race, more so since his breakup with Johanna. His pieces incorporated a larger emphasis on metal work and carvings than Amie's. He still included signature company jewels inlaid into the buckles, bolos and even a few larger necklaces. Each piece also carried the expected Western aura.

Amie was the true artist in the family, but his pieces usually landed well, too. Johanna had always encouraged him to design more....

He scratched his head and leaned back, desk chair squeaking in protest. What had he been thinking, climbing through her window last night like some out-of-control teenager? Except...he had been out of control, jealous over seeing her with his cousin. He hadn't thought. He'd simply acted. That kiss had left him with a need for her that clawed like metal shards scraping his insides raw. Even hearing her voice on the phone forty-five minutes ago had increased the ache of wanting her in his bed again.

A quick buzz from the temp serving as a stand-in personal assistant gave him only a second's warning before his door flung open to reveal Johanna, fire spitting from her eyes. "You missed your flight."

God, she was sexy all riled up.

"I called you." He creaked his chair back even further, taking in the sight of her in white jeans and layered yellow tank tops. "And it's a private plane. *My* private plane, for that matter. There's no way to miss a flight that's waiting for me to give the go-ahead for takeoff."

Speaking of taking off… What he wouldn't give right now to peel away those tanks of hers, one at a time, with his teeth. He'd left her place last night to give himself space to regain control. Instead, their time apart had only taken his need to another level.

"Would have been nice to know you had other plans for your day before I reached the landing strip. I could have worked, too, or slept in. Or…" She held up her hand, four leashes in her fist. "I could have let the dogs play and run around in the yard longer."

She dropped the leashes and the four-pup pack stampeded into his office. Stone barely had time to bark, "Heel, damn it!" before Gem launched into his lap, the full force of the yellow lab almost tipping his chair over. Stone regained his balance then knelt to greet the dogs. Ruby, Sterling and Pearl licked over his face with slobbery wet tongues. He liked animals—clearly, since he'd grown up on a ranch—but these guys in full force were a little much, even for him.

Barks and yips continued until Johanna dipped into sight again, regaining control of the pooches one at time until all four mutts sat in a perfect line. Which only proved she could have controlled them right away. She'd let them overrun him on purpose.

Wincing, he stood, swiping an arm across his face. He shrugged off his suit jacket. Thank goodness he hadn't bothered with a tie today.

He draped his jacket over the back of his leather

chair. "My apologies for inconveniencing you. Even if my grandmother questions my ability to run the company, I do still have obligations here that needed to be taken care of before I could leave."

"Is that what this is about?" She crossed her arms, which threatened to draw his eyes to her chest just when he needed to keep his wits about him and focus on her words. "Showing your grandmother you're indispensable?"

"That's not a nice accusation."

"Is it true?" she pressed.

Damn it, she always saw right through him. But that was only part of the picture. "My primary goal is to bring my grandmother peace. A crisis here at the office will only add to her stress level at a time when she can't afford any additional drain."

Silently, Johanna assessed him through narrowed eyes while the dogs panted, lazy tongues lolling.

"What?" he said. "You don't believe me?"

"I'm skeptical," she said slowly. "Are you still sulking because Alex brought me flowers?"

Did she have to read his every thought? "I don't sulk. I'm charming. Everyone says so."

She cocked an eyebrow. "Yep, you're sure charming the socks off me right now."

Really? He recognized a challenge when he heard one. He flattened a palm to the heavy oak desk that mirrored the one in the ranch office. "If memory serves, I charmed off more than your socks right on this desk about ten months ago."

Her jaw dropped, then clamped shut before she finally said, "Never mind. If you're finished, let's leave so we can get this trip over with sooner rather than later."

All the more reason, in his mind, to prolong this little chat.

She leaned down to gather the leashes.

Kneeling, he clasped her wrist. "Wait, you started this. Let's talk."

"Let's not." She tugged her arm free.

"Fine. Not talking is okay with me, too." Standing, he swept off his desk.

Her eyes went wide. "What are you doing?"

"You said you didn't want to talk." He fingered a button on his shirt. Sure he knew they weren't really going to have sex on his desk, but he reveled in the regret in her eyes that she couldn't hide in spite of her scowl.

She shook her head, blond hair loose and silky sliding along her shoulders. "You're being outrageous."

"Good." He untucked his shirt.

"Stop. Now," she said firmly.

Okay, he'd pushed her far enough for today, but he could see that while their love for each other might have burned out, their passion still had plenty of fire left.

He buttoned his shirt again and tucked in the tails. "Spoilsport."

"Let's clean up the floors first before we go." She brushed papers into a stack. "The pilot's waiting."

"Damn waste of an empty desk." He stacked a haphazard pile of Diamonds in the Rough promo flyers and placed them on the drafting table.

She glanced up at him through long lashes. "Are you trying to chase me off? Because if you don't stop with these stunts, I am out of here. I will place the animals because it's the right thing to do, but you, however, are on your own."

For some reason, her words caught him off guard.

He leaned back against the desk, a weary exhale bursting from him. "Honest to God, Johanna, I don't know what I'm doing. Ever since my grandmother dropped her bombshell, I've just been reacting."

Standing, she clutched a stack of files to her chest, the dog leashes still trailing from her grip. "That's understandable."

"So you're not going to threaten to leave again?" he couldn't stop himself from asking.

She chewed her lip for an instant before responding, "If you keep being honest with me, I will stay."

"Deal." He extended a hand.

She slid hers into his. "Deal."

They stood there with their hands clasped for a few seconds longer than a handshake, seconds that crackled like static in the air just before a thunderstorm.

He enjoyed the hell out of a good drenching downpour, every bit as arousing as a blazing fire.

Her tongue slid along her lips as if to soothe where she'd chewed moments before. His body throbbed in response.

She tugged her hand from his self-consciously and rubbed her fingers along her white jeans. "Where's the first stop on our journey?"

"You don't know?" He would have expected his grandmother to tell her. Yet, even without knowing the specifics, Johanna had signed on for Mariah. That giving spirit was one of the things that had always drawn him to Johanna, even as it simultaneously scared the hell out of him. Because he'd always known she was too good for him. And too wise. Eventually, she would see through him and leave.

He'd been right.

"My grandmother has put me completely at your mercy." He spread his arms wide.

She thrust the leashes at him. "Feels more like I'm at your mercy, but whatever. You can start by helping me with the dogs."

Pivoting away, she strode out of his office, those white jeans showcasing the perfect curve of her hips, her butt. His fist clenched around the leather leads.

Hell, yes, the fire between them was alive and well.

Johanna gripped the leather armrests of her chair during takeoff. The private jet climbed into the sky and she still didn't know where they were going. Yet she'd gotten back into the limousine and onto the plane with Stone and the dogs without demanding more information. She'd been grateful to use the animals as an excuse to end their sexually charged exchange in his office.

Although the confined space of the plane didn't do much to ease the tight knot of desire inside her. The plane leveled out, and she wished her own emotions were as easy to smooth. She sank deeper into the fat chair, its brown leather and brass gleaming.

Each of the pups was now secured in a designer crate bolted to the floor in the back, complete with a luxurious dog bed and a pewter bowl. Engraved nameplates marked each crate and dish. Mariah hadn't been at the landing strip when they returned. Apparently, one set of goodbyes had been as much as she could take. These past two days had been some of the most emotional Johanna had experienced. The only other days that could compare were when her parents had died and when she'd broken her engagement.

And what about Stone? She glanced across the aisle

at him, sympathy whispering through her, mingling with the frustrated passion she'd experienced in his office. Okay, to be frank, that frustrated desire flared every time she saw him, regardless of whether he said outrageous things.

He continued to work, even on the plane, just as he'd been doing when she'd burst into his office earlier. He'd opened his tablet and fired it to life, sitting on the plane's sofa. In days past, she would have curled beside him, close, touching. Now they sat on opposite sides of the jet.

As if he felt her gaze, he spoke without looking up. "We're flying to Vermont to interview a family for Gem first."

"Nice to know you're finally giving specifics for this trip. Please do carry on about Gem, Vermont and this prospective adoptive family."

He flashed a quick dimple without looking up from his tablet. "They have a newborn, so they prefer an adult dog that's already trained."

"They're wise to know that adding a puppy is like having another baby." Sounded promising. "Who's this family?"

"Troy Donavan and his wife, Hillary."

"Donavan?" she repeated in shock. She knew the McNairs had connections, but they acted so down-to-earth sometimes their power still caught her unaware. "The Robin Hood Hacker Donavan? Your grandmother chose a former criminal for her dog?"

"Where's your sense of forgiveness?" He glanced up. "His criminal past was a long time ago. He went to reform school as a teenager."

She snorted on a laugh of disbelief. "For breaking into the Department of Defense computer system. That's more than some teenage prank."

"True," Stone conceded, setting his tablet beside his Stetson. "But he's led a productive and successful life as an adult. Well, once he got past the playboy stage."

"People in glass barns shouldn't throw stones."

"I've missed your humor."

"Thank you."

She'd missed a lot of things about him, which had made her question her decision more than once. Except Stone wasn't known for his forgiving nature. While he'd made it clear he still desired her, she didn't expect he would get over being dumped or change his stance on having children. So all this flirting was counter-productive.

"We're getting off the subject," she said. "Back to the Donavans, please."

"Regardless of Troy's past, all signs indicate the Donavans are a happy couple. But the whole reason for this visit is to be sure Gem is going to a good home. They understand there's no promise the dog will be theirs."

"Good." She nodded tightly. "I have no problem leaving with her if we don't trust them to take the best care of her."

His full-out smile pushed dimples into both cheeks, his skin weathered from the sun. "I've also missed the way you get fearless when it comes to your love of animals. You never were impressed with my money. That's a rare thing."

His genuine compliment moved her as much as his touch and that was dangerous to her peace of mind. "Back to the dogs," she insisted. She pulled a manila folder from her carry-on backpack. "I have questionnaires for the families to fill out to help ensure they are a good fit."

He cocked a dark eyebrow. "A meet and greet is one thing, but you have an adoption application for them to fill out, as well?"

"I prefer the word *questionnaire*," she said primly. "But yes, it could also be called an application."

He leaned back, arms along the sofa. "You do realize they could just buy a dog."

"They could. That doesn't mean we have to give them Gem simply because they have money. If anything, adopting Gem will show their child that love can't be bought." Tapping the folder, she sighed sadly. "It's becoming clear now that your grandmother was right to send me with you."

"What if they're awesome but Gem isn't a good fit or doesn't like them? How will you explain it to them?" he asked, appearing to be genuinely interested. "What will you tell my grandmother?"

"Your grandmother will understand. That was her reason for sending us rather than just shipping the dogs directly to the families."

"And the Donavans?" he pushed for more.

That would be awkward but not enough to make her go against her principles. "I will suggest they go to their local animal shelter to find a forever furry friend." She couldn't resist adding, "Hopefully, they'll make a huge donation while they're there."

"You've thought a lot through since just yesterday."

She rolled her shoulders in a shrug. "I'm also trusting you to roll out that charisma to smooth over any rough patches if need be."

"Somehow I don't think you're complimenting me."

Were his feelings really hurt? He seemed so confident most—all—of the time. She unbuckled and walked across the aisle to sit beside him and oops, she hadn't given much thought to the fact that his arms were extended along the couch, which in effect put his arm around her.

She held herself upright to keep from leaning into his hold. "Why don't you just keep Gem? Didn't some client give him to you?"

"He's not really mine. He may have been given to me, but he always preferred my grandmother." He picked up a lock of her hair. "Truth is, Gem was a gift from a guy who had the hots for my grandmother and was trying to wrangle an in with the family, since she loves dogs."

"Run that by me again?" How had she not known that?

"After my grandfather died of a heart attack, a lot of guys made moves on Gran," he said darkly. "She was a rich widow. Pretty. Guys were lining up. Some were genuine," he conceded. "Some were fortune hunters."

"Yet she never remarried."

"She says no one matches up to my grandfather."

Johanna's parents had felt the same way about each other. She wanted a love like that for herself and she wasn't willing to settle. "That's sweet and sad at the same time, loving that much and losing it."

He shifted in his seat. "Back to the story of how we got Gem as a puppy…"

"Not so at ease with the emotional stuff, are you?" How many other times had he dodged speaking about deeper feelings when she'd just assumed he was jaded or insensitive?

"Puppy. Gem." His firm voice made it clear he wasn't

taking her bait. He would stay in control of the conversation, going only as far as he decided to go.

"This guy thought he was being original giving me a dog to get to my grandmother. Little did he know, he wasn't the first dude to try that. The first guy brought a puppy—Gem number one—when I was around nine. The guy who'd given him to me to get to my grandmother... Boy, did that ever backfire on him. The puppy hated kids, had zero interest in playing ball or sleeping at the foot of my bed. He just wanted to go on lazy walks, which sounded boring to me at that age."

An image unfolded in her head of Stone as a little boy. And what little boy wouldn't be thrilled over a puppy? How sad he must have been to have the first Gem ignore him, reject him. He wouldn't have understood.

She leaned toward his hand ever so slightly as he toyed with her hair. "That's why all the family members should meet a pet first before deciding on the best fit for their family. Otherwise, it's not fair to the dog or the people."

"So the guy learned as my grandmother showed him the door." He wrapped the lock of hair around his finger as the jet engines hummed in the background. "The guy offered to drop the puppy off at the local shelter, which was totally the wrong thing to say to my grandmother. She dumped the guy flat and kept the puppy for herself." He smiled fondly at the memory, his gaze shifting to the yellow Labrador asleep in her crate. "So the next time a guy brought a puppy trying to win Gran over, we named him Gem II. Both Gems were her favorite walking companions."

Affection for his grandmother wrapped around his

every word. Saying goodbye to Gem would start that letting go, the beginning of a grieving process Johanna wished she could take from him or make easier. Even thinking about all the pain he would face watching his grandmother's health fail squeezed at Johanna's heart.

Before she could stop the impulse, she wrapped her arms around Stone.

Five

Kissing Johanna had rocked his world, always had. But since they'd begun this trip, he'd been the one to make the first move each time they'd touched. Having Johanna reach for him sent Stone rocketing into another orbit altogether.

He didn't need any further encouragement.

Sliding his arms around her, he breathed in her flowery scent and savored the silky tease of her braided hair gripped in his fist. The plane engines hummed an echo of the desire buzzing through his veins.

And to think, he'd almost messed this up.

His first instinct when she'd offered consolation had been to shrug off her sympathy. Then his better sense had kicked in. He had Johanna in his arms. Touching him. Sighing.

He skimmed a hand down her pulled-back hair, releasing more of that floral scent. Her slim body molded to him, the softness of her breasts against his chest so familiar. So damn perfect. He nuzzled her ear, right beside the filigreed dream catcher dangling from her lobe. Her arms tightened around him, her hand cupping his neck. Just the feel of being skin to skin sent his heart slugging against his ribs.

Her fingers stroked through his hair, and he couldn't hold back any longer. He kissed her, fully and thoroughly, with his mouth, his hands, his body. From the first time he'd touched her and tasted her, desire had pulsed through him. Stronger than any attraction he'd ever experienced. He'd known then. Johanna was special.

For years he'd seen her as only that kid wandering around the stable yard. Everything had changed the day she'd come riding in after getting caught in a rainstorm. Her clothes had been plastered to her body. He'd gathered a couple of towels to give her. Two pats in and he'd known. He'd wanted her.

Still did.

That had been two years ago, a couple of years after she'd finished vet tech school and taken a job at the Hidden Gem Ranch. A year later they'd been engaged. Five months later, she'd returned his ring.

His mind shied away from that part and back to the passion, the connection, the need. He stroked along her spine until he reached the waistband of her jeans. Her layered tank tops had ridden up to expose a patch of skin. He palmed her waist, drawing her closer. She wriggled nearer, her fingers gripping his hair, her mouth moving along his, meeting him kiss for kiss, touch for touch.

She might have only meant to console him, but she was clearly every bit as moved as he was by the moment. She wanted him every bit as much as he wanted her. There wasn't a question in his mind.

He reclined her onto the sofa, stretching out over her. Her long legs twined with his. A husky moan vibrated in her throat. Her head fell back and she arched into the press of his mouth as he kissed down her neck.

Tucking a hand between them, he slid the button free on her jeans, then flicked her belly button ring. His thumb recognized the jewelry from touch, a tiny silver boot with spurs and a diamond stud at the top. Possessiveness stirred deep in his gut. He'd given it to her early in their relationship, when she'd still wanted to keep their connection a secret. She'd been nervous about people calling her an opportunist.

That she still wore the gift stoked his passion and made him bolder. He eased her zipper down link by link then dipped his hand inside. He knew the feel of her, had memorized every inch of her, but after months without her, there was also a newness to this moment. He slipped his fingers lower, lower still until he found...

Yes.

The slick proof of her arousal set his skin on fire. Her hips rolled as she surrendered to his touch. Her husky, needy whispers caressed his ears.

Her hands roved his back restlessly, her nails scoring a needy path down his spine, tugging the hem of his shirt from his suit pants. With a frenzied yank, she popped the buttons of his shirt. He pushed up her tank tops, and bare flesh met bare flesh, damn near sending him over the edge.

This was getting out of control fast. The pilot was a simple door away. Stone had hoped to steal a kiss but he hadn't dared hope things would go this far. He needed to ensure their privacy. The sleeping area in back was small but plenty sufficient to make thorough love to her. He'd done so more than once as he'd sought to romance her around the world.

Easing his hand from her jeans with more than a little regret over losing her sweetness for even a brief break, he rolled from her, keeping his mouth sealed to hers. He tucked both arms under Johanna and lifted her against his chest. More than once he'd carried her to bed or to his desk or to a field of bluebonnets. On this realm, at least, they were in perfect synch with one another.

"Stone—" she nipped his ear with a husky sigh "—you have to know this isn't a wise idea, but for some reason I can't bring myself to say no."

"I never claimed anything about our relationship was logical." He shouldered open the door to the jet's sleeping quarters.

She cupped his face in her hands. "What do you mean by that?"

He adjusted his hold on her as he neared the bed covered in a thick comforter. Dim pot lights overhead illuminated the small jet cabin. "I've always known that you are too good for me. It was only a matter of time until you figured it out."

Her forehead furrowed. "Is that really how you felt, or are you manipulating me because I'm having a weak moment?"

Manipulating her? Is that what she really thought of him?

Her words splashed cold reality over him. This wasn't the right time to take her back into his bed again. He'd made considerable progress just now and he didn't intend to lose ground by pushing for too much too soon. If he slept with her now, she might never trust him enough for a second time…and hell, yes, he knew once would not be enough.

He lowered her feet to the ground. The glide of her

body against his made him throb all the harder, almost changing his mind and to hell with wisdom. He wanted—needed—her now so damn much his teeth ached.

Almost.

"You'll have to decide that for yourself." He backed away, his hands up between them, trying to keep his eyes firmly focused on her face rather than on the gorgeous tangled mess of her hair and the open vee of her jeans. "And when you do, if you still want us to sleep together again, just say the word and I'll be there before you can say 'let's get naked.' But I need to know you're in one hundred percent, no regrets."

He pivoted away and out the door before he made a liar out of himself and tangled up in the sheets with her for what he knew would be the best sex of their lives.

Five hours later, in Vermont, Johanna's brain was still spinning with confusion after how close she'd come to sleeping with Stone again.

Sleeping? More like unraveling in his arms at just one touch.

At least she had the distraction of a picnic lunch with the Donavan family while she gathered her thoughts. She and Stone had brought Gem along to meet them, while the other three dogs unwound in a fenced area around the guesthouse where Stone and Johanna would be staying tonight.

The late lunch with the Donavan family was an intriguing surprise. Johanna sat at a rustic picnic table while Hillary Donavan pushed her snoozing infant son in a baby swing under a sprawling sugar maple tree. Hillary was so down-to-earth she could have been Jo-

hanna's redheaded cousin, complete with freckles and
a high swinging ponytail. Johanna felt at ease, something she hadn't expected once she'd heard who they
would be visiting first.

Hillary's husband was every bit as approachable in
spite of his notorious history as the Robin Hood hacker.
Wearing a fedora with his khaki shorts and T-shirt,
Troy ran alongside Stone playing fetch with Gem in a
field of red clover.

The Donavan homestead was as understated as the
couple. A 1920s farmhouse perched on a low rolling
hill. A porch wrapped around the first floor and black
shutters bracketed the windows.

Bit by bit she saw the amenities added into the landscape so artfully she'd barely noticed. A pool nestled
near a wooded area with rock ledges and a waterfall
gave it the appearance of a stream feeding into a pond—
a clear, chlorinated pond. A child's playhouse had been
built from wood under a massive tree. A security fence
enclosed the entire two-acre property—which enabled
her to check a box on the adoption application. A lab
like Gem would need a safe place to run out her energy
with this wonderful family.

She sipped her iced tea, finally beginning to relax
now that part one of their mission appeared to be a success. The lunch together had been just what Johanna
needed to unwind after the tension of the past twenty-
four hours. The meal had been beyond delicious without
being overly elaborate. A juicy fruit salad accompanied
loaves of hearty peasant bread and deli meats, cheeses
and spreads of their choice. Fresh-squeezed lemonade.
And the ice cream… Her mouth watered as she finished
off another bite of fresh maple walnut ice cream. These

parents were clearly trying to give their child as normal a life as possible, given little T.J.—Troy Junior—was the offspring of one of the wealthiest men in the world.

Hillary wrapped her arms around her knees as she hitched her feet up onto the bench by the redwood picnic table. "We appreciate you going to so much trouble to bring Gem to us. He's such a great dog, playful but well trained."

"Thank *you* for letting us invade your home. We could have met in a park or somewhere generic for you to see Gem."

"I loved time at the park as a child, but I'm still nervous about taking T.J. out in public for security reasons." Hillary's hand fell protectively to stroke the baby's head.

The Donavan compound clearly had top-of-the-line security that could rival Fort Knox, including computerized keypads discreetly hidden and staff that could have doubled as bouncers. Johanna had never thought about the safety issue with Stone's upbringing. How difficult it must have been for his family to balance all that wealth with values. He'd clearly been born into a vast dynasty, but he had a strong work ethic. She'd always admired that about him.

Apparently, the Donavans felt the same.

"Well, Hillary, I have to say this is definitely more comfy than a park. It's generous of you to host us overnight."

The thought of being alone with Stone tonight was starting to sink in. Her skin tingled at the notion.

Hillary's gaze scanned the low rolling hills around their home. "We bought this place to give T.J. the kind of upbringing neither of us had."

Johanna angled her head to the side. "Where did you grow up?"

"Here in Vermont actually, but much more scaled back and…well…not secure." She looked back at Johanna. "I love my mom, but she was troubled. Actually, she was an alcoholic. It took us a long time to reconcile, but I'm glad we found a way to make peace before she passed."

"Oh, um, I'm sorry you had to go through that," she said, feeling totally inadequate. *Sorry* was such a lame, overused word. "Is the rest of your family still nearby?"

"My sister, yes. Troy and I have extended family, as well, the kinds of friends that are as close as relatives. We visit each other as often as we can, but we all bought vacation homes in Monte Carlo so our kids can have a sense of growing up together like cousins."

Hillary's shoulders lost much of their tension at the mention of her husband's close friends, and she launched into a story about their most recent trip to Monaco for a Formula One racing event.

The baby boy squawked awake in his swing, stopping Hillary midstory. With already expert hands, she scooped up her newborn and declared, "He needs changing and I didn't bring enough diapers out here. If you'll excuse me for a few minutes, I'll be right back."

"Of course. Take your time. I'm enjoying the sunshine." And trying so very hard not to be envious of Hillary's glowing happiness.

As if to rub salt in the wound in her aching heart, Troy noticed his wife's departure and took off after her in a slow jog, Gem loping alongside him having already transferred his doggy allegiance to the Donavans.

Stone peeled away and strode back toward her, so

damn handsome he took her breath away. Yet she knew even if he turned gray and paunchy, the essence of the man would be the same.

Strong. Driven. Accomplished. Charismatic.

And still determined to deny himself—both of them—the family happiness she craved. As much as she wanted him, she couldn't bring herself to settle for less than everything.

Taking a seat beside Johanna at the picnic table, Stone saw the wistfulness in her eyes as she watched the family tableau. He knew, without question, he'd put that pain there. Guilt threatened to drive him to his knees.

This whole afternoon of domestic bliss had been tough for him, as well, reminding him of all the times he'd seen his cousins with their parents while he sat on the periphery. He'd moved past wanting that for himself and realized he was better off not inflicting the same disappointment on offspring of his own. He knew his limitations. He didn't have the emotional capacity to be a parent, and he refused to let down a kid. A parent had to be 100 percent in. Otherwise it wasn't fair to the child. Johanna would expect—and deserved—to have a spouse every bit as committed to home and hearth as she was, rather than some stonehearted guy with a crack baby past.

He didn't want to think overlong about the man who would offer her that fairy-tale future, especially not with the feel and taste of Johanna still so fresh in his memory. The sun kissed her shoulders, which were bared in her sundress. He allowed himself at least a small indulgence and grazed his knuckles along the tanned skin, sweeping aside her golden French braid.

He cupped the back of her neck and massaged lightly. "Are you okay with the Donavans adopting Gem?"

"What do you think?" Her head lolled back into his touch. "I'm thrilled. Gem is going to a wonderful family. There's nothing not to love about this."

"I have to confess, it's going even better than I'd hoped." His thumb worked at a knotted muscle at the base of her skull. The silkiness of her skin and the light sigh passing her lips stirred him.

Her eyelids fluttered closed, her face a study in bliss. "Your grandmother will be relieved to hear the news."

"I already texted her." He waggled his cell phone before tucking it away again.

"You what?" Her emerald-green eyes snapped open, surprise and a hint of something else sparking. "That was mighty confident of you. What if I'd disagreed? I am a part of this process, you know."

"I could tell you were okay with this about thirty minutes in." His thumb brushed along her cheek before returning to the back of her neck again. "I may not be the right man for you, but I know you well."

She swatted at his chest lightly. "Then why did you bother asking when you sat down with me a few minutes ago?"

"It was an excuse to talk to you, and God knows, I wasn't going to pass up an opportunity to touch you." His voice went gravelly. His self-control was shot around her these days.

Her chest rose and fell faster in a tangible mirror of his arousal. "Why are you torturing us both this way?"

Hell if he knew the answer. "How about we both just enjoy the outdoors and sunshine? We have red clover instead of bluebonnets, but the love of the land is still here. Nothing is going to happen between us out here in the open, especially not with the Donavans nearby. There's no harm. Accept the neck massage and relax."

Some of the anger melted from her kinked muscles and she sagged back into his touch. "You always did give the best neck rubs."

"It's been a stressful couple of days." He hadn't wanted to leave Texas and now he couldn't envision what life would be like after they returned. "I sent my grandmother photos of Gem with the Donavans."

"That was thoughtful of you."

"She texted back that she's happy and relieved." And he had to confess knowing he'd eased that worry for her made him as happy as if he'd landed a big new contract. "So yes, our task is twenty-five percent complete."

"I know those photos must have brought Mariah a lot of joy." Angling toward him, Johanna stroked along his eyebrows before cupping his face. Her fingertips were callused from work, but gentle, soothing, the hands of a healer. "We may not be meant to be married, but there was—is—so much about you that's special. Otherwise I never could have fallen for you."

"Yet, here we are."

Silence settled between them, highlighting nature's sounds of branches rustling in the wind and birds chirping.

Johanna's eyes went sad, unshed tears glistening. "I wish things could be different for us, I truly do."

He agreed 100 percent. But where did that leave them? "We haven't talked about what happened between us earlier on the airplane."

"What *almost* happened," she amended.

"Right." That sure put him in his place. Still, he

couldn't stop the urge to indulge in a week of no-strings sex, to make the most of one last chance to be with Johanna. "Do you still feel like I was trying to manipulate you?"

She eased back, her hand falling from his face, and she ducked her head to avoid his touch. "Nothing's changed. We both know an affair can't lead anywhere."

"Not even a temporary fling," he said in a joke, though he was more than half-serious.

She didn't laugh. But she didn't say no, either. She simply sat in silence as the wind sent a couple of stray maple leaves skittering across the picnic table.

Hope surged through him along with a pulse of heat in his veins. He knew they couldn't have a long-term relationship, but he could feel her giving in to this week together. He pressed ahead. He just had to figure out what was holding her back. "Is there someone else?"

She choked on a laugh. "Are you serious? I live on your land, and I work at your family's ranch. There aren't any secrets."

No secrets? She was wrong there. He'd been clueless about Alex's feelings for her. "My cousin has a thing for you, and I didn't know about that."

She crossed her arms over her chest, plumping the gentle curves of her breasts along the neckline of her yellow sundress. "I told you there's nothing between Alex and me."

"But he wants there to be more." Stone's jaw clenched at the thought of her with someone else. The possibility that someone could be his cousin, and that Stone would have to watch them together every day for the rest of his life, was still more than he could wrap his brain around without blowing a gasket. "That's clear to me now. Although why I didn't see it earlier is a mystery."

"I can't control what your cousin feels, but I can assure you those feelings are not returned." She touched his wrist lightly, tentatively. "This isn't Alex's fault. People don't always make wise choices about who to... be drawn to."

"Are you talking about us now?"

Chuckling wryly, she squeezed his hand. "You truly are clueless if you even have to ask. No wonder you didn't notice how Alex feels."

Even though she insisted she didn't want Alex, Stone still had to know more. "How far did things go with Alex before you realized you weren't interested in him that way?"

For a moment, he thought she would refuse to answer his question, but then her shoulders lowered, defensiveness melting from her. Her answer was important to him, too important. His heart pounded in his ears.

"Alex asked me out once. I said no, because I'm not into rebound relationships. I also didn't want to cause trouble between the two of you."

"You care about both of us," he realized. How much did she care about Alex? Was she holding back?

"Of course I care about you both." Her hand stayed on his. Did she know her thumb stroked along his wrist? "I practically grew up on the ranch with both of you. In fact, I played more with Alex and Amie since they're younger than you. Of course I spent a lot more time studying you because of my monster crush. Sometimes it amazes me how I can know so much about you in some ways and so little in others."

He flipped his hand over to grip hers. "We saw what we wanted to see."

"I know you and Alex are as close as brothers. The last thing I want to do is cause trouble between you."

"We don't always see eye to eye on everything, but we're close. We'll get through this, too." The thought of losing any more of his family was beyond considering. "We grew up like brothers."

Except they weren't, in spite of all the times he'd wished they could be.

"You guys definitely had troublemaker moments." She grinned, lightening the mood and taking them back to safer ground. "Remember when the two of you put Kool-Aid in Amie's showerhead right before the Miss Stampede Queen pageant? I didn't think she would ever forgive either of you for turning her hair pink."

"That was Alex's idea."

"Um, I don't think so. And if it was, that's probably because you whispered the idea in his ear when he was sleeping."

Or because he'd left a gag book open to a particular page right on Alex's desk. Stone grinned. "I may have instigated some—okay, *most* of the pranks." He recognized her attempt to get off the subject and he didn't intend to lose sight of what he needed to know.

"Both of you were fantasy material for all my school friends—rich, sexy cowboys. What's not to drool over?" Mischief sparkled in her eyes. "But as you know, my crush was firmly placed on you."

"What about now?"

The pool filter kicked on, the fountain spewing higher. He looked over his shoulder and found staff clearing away the dishes discreetly. Once they left, Johanna leaned toward him again.

"You and I are not engaged anymore, and our core reason for the breakup hasn't changed. You know that," she said gently but firmly.

"Yet, we were kissing a few hours ago." Kissing and more.

She pulled her hand back. "This kind of conversation is exactly what I wanted to avoid."

"If I weren't in the picture, would you and Alex be together?" He hated the way this discussion made him feel, the jealousy, the doubts. But damn it, he couldn't let it go.

Her lips went tight with frustration for an instant. "I've already told you I'm not seeing Alex."

"I heard you." He remembered everything she'd ever said to him. "I'm asking if you have romantic feelings for him. That's different."

She shoved to her feet, walking absently toward the trunk of the maple tree before glancing back over her shoulder. "You're not going to let this go, are you?"

"You broke up with me, not the other way around." And the days following that breakup had been some of the darkest in his life.

"Your cousin and I are very much alike." She sagged against the trunk. "Too much so to be a couple."

His shoulders dropped with relief. "I'm glad to hear that...." He stood and walked to her, grabbing a branch just over her head. "Even though I know I have no rights, the thought of you being with him drives me crazy."

"Is that why you made a move on me at my place, in your office—on the plane?"

"I kissed you because I wanted to." Like now.

"And that's the first time you've wanted to in seven months?"

"Hell, no." He thought about having her every day—and every night.

"Then something changed to make you act on the impulse. Is that 'something' jealousy?" Her eyes searched him with genuine confusion. "If you can't have me, no one can?"

Put that way, he sounded like a jerk. "I don't know how to explain it other than to say that since my grandmother dropped her bombshell news on us, it feels like the world is off-kilter."

"So if your grandmother was healthy, you would still be keeping your distance, like before."

Was she hinting that she'd wanted him to fight harder to get her back? One wrong move and he could wreck the moment. The only thing he knew to do was be honest.

"Hell, I don't even really know what I mean except that we are here, together. And the thought of never being with you again is tearing me apart."

She swallowed hard, chewing her bottom lip as she stared up at him.

Stone continued, "I also know I can't just stand around and pretend to be unaffected. So either leave now or prepare to be fully, thoroughly kissed."

"I, I just... I can't." She stuttered, shaking her head slowly, sidestepping away from the tree, then rushing past him.

She couldn't be any clearer than that.

Disappointment delivered a kick to the gut even though he hadn't expected anything different.

He gave her enough time to make it inside before he released the tree branch and started back toward the main house. He only had an afternoon and dinnertime to get his head together before they spent the night alone together in the guesthouse.

One afternoon didn't sound like nearly long enough when even seven months hadn't helped him get over Johanna.

Johanna had busied herself caring for the other three dogs, taking them on a hike, feeding them, hiking again, and still restless energy whirled inside her well into suppertime.

Their evening was coming to an end with coffee on the covered back porch, a lazy ceiling fan rustling the air. Soon, she wouldn't be able to hide behind the Donavan family any longer. She would be spending the night alone with Stone.

Of course she could go to a hotel. Nothing in Mariah's agreement said she had to sleep under the same roof as Stone. She just had to help him place the dogs. Except she didn't want to cause an embarrassing scene for him in front of the Donavans....

Oh, hell, who was she kidding? She wanted to finish their afternoon conversation and learn more about why he was pursuing her now. He'd said his grandmother's terminal illness had flipped his world. If he was reevaluating, could he change his mind on things that had kept them apart before?

If so, could she trust her heart to him a second time?

Walking away the first time had nearly destroyed her with grief and loss. They were barely a day into this trip and her willpower was fading fast. She finished the last of her iced decaf coffee.

Stone set aside his empty mug and leaned toward Johanna. "We should say our good-nights. Do you have the gift from my grandmother?"

"Oh, right." She jolted and reached into her woven satchel. "We have a present for your son, to thank you both for having us here and for giving Gem a good home."

She pulled out a Diamonds in the Rough gift sack and passed it to Hillary. The bag glistened with the pattern of diamonds and spurs, the company's bold, black logo scrolled at an angle.

"How thoughtful," Troy said. "You didn't have to do this, but thanks. Hillary, how about you do the honors."

"I do love surprises." She passed over the snoozing infant to Stone.

A momentary panic flashed in his eyes, quickly masked before he cradled the baby carefully in his arms. His broad hands cupped the tiny bottom and supported the head. His sun-bronzed skin contrasted with the newborn alabaster of the baby.

Johanna's heart melted. How could it not? Her fondest dream in her heart of hearts was playing out in front of her. Stone rocked the baby in his arms as if by instinct. A lump lodged in her throat as big as the welling emotion filling her heart.

She vaguely registered the sound of rustling paper as Hillary unwrapped the gift they'd brought. Stone's gaze flew to Johanna's and held. The rawness in his eyes tore at her. She saw…pain. She saw a hurt so deep she ached to reach out and wrap her arms around him.

Clearing his throat, Stone pivoted away and passed

the baby back to Troy. Johanna shook off the daze and looked at Hillary again.

The baby's mother pulled out a box, untied the fat orange ribbon and pulled out… "A tiny rodeo buckle! How adorable."

Hillary held up the tot-sized leather belt with a rodeo buckle, the leather crafted and studded with one of Amie's originals. It was a one-of-a-kind design with a cartoon horse and baby cowboy engraved on the pewter oval.

Stone picked up the bag and tucked the box inside. "He'll have to grow a bit for it to fit."

"Thank you," Hillary said, tracing the design with her finger. "This is fabulous. We'll be sure to take a photo of him wearing it and playing with Gem."

Troy held the baby in one arm like a seasoned dad, clapping Stone on the shoulder with his other hand. "Thank you again for thinking of us for Gem. He's a great dog. And you're welcome to visit him anytime."

Stone nodded tightly. "Thank you for giving her a good home and easing my grandmother's mind."

Johanna's heart ached all over again for Stone. No wonder he was having a tougher time hiding his feelings. If they'd still been a couple, she could have comforted him, even if all he would let her do was hold his hand.

She couldn't help but be reminded of when he was about twenty-one or twenty-two and his favorite horse had gone lame. Even with the best vets money could bring, nothing could be done to save Jet. She'd found Stone grieving in the stable with his horse afterward. She'd just been a gangly teenager and hugging him would have been out of the question regardless. So she'd just sat beside him quietly, being there. He hadn't asked her to leave, and she liked to think her presence had made things somewhat easier for him.

God knew, Stone would need someone now as he dealt with his grandmother's illness, and he'd always made a point of being stoic, as if the problems rolled right off him. Mariah had been the most important person in his life, the only parental figure he'd had after his grandfather had passed away while Stone was still young.

Hillary smiled gently, tucking the belt back into the bag. "It's our pleasure to have Gem as a part of our family. He will be T.J.'s best buddy and a treasured friend." She patted Stone on the arm, seeming to understand that was as much tenderness as the man would accept right now. "The guest cabin is fully stocked with food and drinks, but please let us know if you need anything at all. Otherwise we'll see you after breakfast to say goodbye before you leave."

In the morning?

Johanna's heart leaped to her throat. Of course it was time to call an end to the evening and go to the guesthouse. Resisting Stone had been difficult enough when occasionally crossing paths at the ranch. But tonight, with the memory of him cradling that tiny infant in his powerful arms?

She didn't know how she would hold strong once the doors closed behind them.

Six

Johanna's stomach tightened with each step closer to the guesthouse. A barn perched on a hill behind the Donavan's main home had been converted into a guesthouse with soaring ceilings. One side had been removed and replaced with glass windows.

Tonight, she and Stone would sleep under the same roof together for the first time in seven months. They walked side-by-side silently, not touching. But the wind twined around them as if binding them with whispering bands of air carrying his scent mingling with hers.

The desire that still simmered between them was out in the open now. Discussed. Acknowledged. She'd told him no, and he'd respected that. But to be honest with herself, she wasn't so certain she could hold out through tonight, much less through this whole week without succumbing to the temptation of one last fling. One more chance to lose herself in being with him. To immerse herself in total bliss. If only they didn't have to face the morning.

Once the guesthouse door closed behind them, there would be no more delaying. And she was feeling all the more vulnerable after watching him hold the Donavan baby. The evening seemed to have been tailor-made to play with her emotions.

Stone opened the gate to the picket fence around the guesthouse. Cuddly Sterling, impish Pearl and loyal Ruby raced up to greet them, barking and sniffing their hands. Little Pearl's head tipped to the side quizzically.

Crouching, Johanna scratched the cairn terrier's head. "It's as if she's asking about Gem. I wish there was a way to keep them all together. I have to admit I'm going to miss that goof of a dog."

"Life doesn't always work out the way we'd hoped and we're just left with doing the best we can." Stone ruffled the Rottweiler's ears, then the dachshund mix's. "Thank goodness Mariah made sure all her dogs and cats were placed in good homes."

Johanna glanced up through her eyelashes at Stone. His broad shoulders against the sentimental moonlight made for a mouth-watering silhouette. "You're right. I'm just…feeling emotional about Mariah. I know it must be so much worse for you."

He cricked his neck from side to side. "Let's get through the week as best we can."

"Of course, there's satisfaction to be found in doing something tangible for Mariah." She scooped up the dachshund. Seven-year-old Sterling cuddled closer as if sensing the ache inside her. "We should, uh, turn in. We have a lot of ground to cover this week for the other dogs."

Nerves pattered as quickly as racing dog feet as she made fast tracks along the pavers toward the guesthouse.

Stone followed—she could hear the steady even tread of his long-legged stride. He reached past her, thumbed in the security code and pushed the large door wide into the sweeping great room.

Pearl and Ruby raced past, sniffing and exploring, closing in on the large dog bowl of water even though they'd had plenty to drink outside, as well. She set Sterling down to join them. Three fat, fluffy dog beds were lined up behind the sofa. The Donavans were thoughtful hosts.

As she turned toward the expansive glass wall, she couldn't help but think the winter must be magnificent with the view of a snow-covered countryside. Even now, the sight was beyond magnificent, lush and green with cows grazing. She worked with large animals as a vet tech every day and had seen farms across Texas, but even she found this place breathtaking. What would it be like to have visited these people when she and Stone had been a couple? Most of their outings had been to more pretentious social gatherings, high-end fund-raisers or business functions.

Nothing like this day or this place.

The Donavans clearly had embraced the Vermont experience, complete with dairy cows. Although not all Vermont farms came with an ice cream parlor just for their kids.

Stone whistled softly from the state-of-the-art kitchen. "When they said they'd stocked the kitchen for us, they weren't joking. Do you want something to drink? Just pick, I'm sure it's here. Snacks, breakfast pastries, fruit and ice cream. Holy cow—so to speak."

Listening to him ramble off the flavors, she realized he was doing his best to ease the tension between them. Definitely a wise idea if she wanted to get through this week with her sanity intact. "I'll take a scoop of the maple nut."

"Coming right up," he said, opening cabinets and drawers.

She walked to the kitchen island and hitched a hip up onto a bar stool. "They're a surprisingly normal family, given all their wealth."

He passed her a bowl and spoon. "Are you saying that my family is pretentious because of our money?"

"Not at all. But some of your friends…" She stabbed her spoon into the generous mound of ice cream in the blue stoneware bowl. "They looked right through my father in the stables."

Scowling, he stood across from her, his bowl in front of him. "I'm sorry to hear that."

"You were more than just sorry about it," she answered, remembering well how he'd stood up to snobs. "You did something about it. I remember this one time when I was about eleven and one of your college friends was ordering my dad around. You made sure that guy was given the slowest, least cooperative horse in the stable. The horse even sat in the middle of a stream and got the guy soaking wet. I knew it wasn't accidental on your part. Was it?"

He winked, his scowl fading. "You seem to have me all figured out."

"You always treated everyone with respect." Her trip down memory lane reminded her of the reasons she'd fallen for this man in the first place. "You took care of your own horse. But that day when I was eleven, I officially developed my crush on you."

"You never told me that story before." He shoveled a spoonful of ice cream into his mouth, his eyes tracking her every movement with an intensity that tingled through her.

"I had insecurities of my own in those days," she admitted now. It was tough to share her self-doubts around someone as confident and, yes, arrogant as Stone. "I was a tomboy, freckled and gangly, living in a trailer park. I was brought up with strong values and I loved my parents, the life they made for me."

"They loved you. The pride on your dad's face when he talked about you was unmistakable."

"Thank you…" Her eyes misted just thinking about them. She understood all too well the pain Stone was facing, losing his mother figure. "I miss them so much, especially lately."

He ate silently, letting her find her way through. She wasn't sure where her thoughts were taking her, but she felt the need to make him understand something she couldn't quite define herself.

Johanna set her spoon aside. "I know your family is full of good people, open-minded and generous. A part of me didn't want to show just how vulnerable I felt. Even growing up on the ranch, I was on the periphery as an employee's child."

She shook her head, her voice trailing off, and she ate a bite of ice cream to cover her silence. The maple flavor melted over her taste buds.

"Johanna…" He clasped her wrist. "Go ahead. I'm listening."

Licking the spoon clean, ever aware of his eyes on her mouth, she gathered her words. "It's strange how you said you felt you weren't good enough for me…. Learning which fork to use for an occasional meal at the big house is a long way from walking in billionaire circles on a day-to-day basis. Keeping up appearances during our engagement and constantly worrying I would do something to embarrass you was exhausting."

"You never let it show." His frown turned to a scowl. "Don't you think that's something I would have cared to know? We were engaged to be married, for God's sake. If we couldn't tell each other even something basic like that, then what did we even have together?"

"You're angry?"

"I'm frustrated, yes. All this time I've been thinking that I let you down." He shoved aside his bowl and leaned on his elbows, closing the space between them. "Right now, I'm realizing we let each other down. Except you weren't interested in shouldering your part of the blame."

Anger sparked along her already raw nerves. "I open up to you, and now you're pissed off? That isn't very fair."

He sidestepped around the island to stand in front of her. "Nothing about what has happened between us has been fair or we wouldn't still be hurting this much."

She swallowed hard, certain to her toes he was about to kiss her and she wouldn't be able to tell him no. They would pour all those frustrated emotions into passion. It wouldn't solve anything, but at least they would have an outlet, a release.

Except he turned and left.

Her jaw dropped.

What the hell? Stone had just walked away from her?

She almost leaped from her seat to charge after him and demand he finish the conversation. How dare he just leave? They had unfinished business....

But hadn't she done the same thing to him? Not only had she run away from him after the picnic, scared she couldn't resist the temptation to do more than kiss him. But she'd also walked out on their relationship and very publicly, at that. His words settled in her gut along with the sting of guilt. He was right. She'd let him shoulder all the blame for their breakup when she hadn't given her all to him, either.

The realization echoed hollowly inside her. She gathered both bowls and rinsed them out carefully, wishing her confusion was as easily swirled down the drain. Or that she could just shake off her worries and go to sleep like the three dogs curled up on their beds, snoring. The thought of going to her room alone was more than she could bear tonight after watching all-day family bliss with the Donavans, not just as parents but as a couple.

She yanked a blanket from the back of the sofa and curled up on the couch to count stars instead of sheep.

Stone woke the next morning with a throbbing headache and an aching erection.

His shower took care of the visible sign of his arousal, but didn't do much to cool the fire inside him. Walking away from Johanna the night before had been one of the most difficult things he'd ever done. But he'd been too angry, too on edge. He didn't trust himself and damned if he would ever put her at risk.

So he'd left her alone. He'd worked for hours before falling into a fitful sleep just before sunup.

Tossing his shaving gear into his bag, he was still steamed over his conversation with Johanna last night. He'd spent most of the night reviewing their time together and he kept coming back to how she'd broken up with him at one of his grandmother's major fundraisers. That couldn't be coincidental. If he'd known how she'd felt, he could have done things differently. Hell, he could have—

What? Given up his job and all the responsibilities that came with that? Dismissed his background and offered to give her the family she wanted? Last night he'd learned of yet another reason they weren't meant to be together.

Who would he be if he didn't run Diamonds in the Rough?

He tossed his bag on the thick four-poster bed beside a stack of discarded sketches for a new kids' line with a horse logo. The images just wouldn't come together on paper the way he saw them in his mind. Visions of a misty-eyed Johanna kept interfering, thoughts of her struggling to hold back tears when he'd held the baby.

Damn it.

He flipped open his suitcase, pulled out a pair of well-worn jeans and tugged them on. One day into this mandated week together and he was already losing his damn mind. He scratched his hands through his wet hair, needing to get his head together.

Barring that, he could at least let the dogs out.

He opened his bedroom door, wondering if Johanna was up yet. He didn't hear her so he assumed not. The wide-open barn space sprawled in front of him. The dogs sat up, one, two, three—tails wagging, tongues lolling out. They launched off their beds behind the sofa in unison but thank God, not barking. He knelt, petting each to keep them quiet. Then he snapped his fingers to lead them to the door. Walking past the couch, he almost stopped short. Johanna slept on the sofa, wrapped in a quilt, still wearing her sundress from yesterday.

His gaze stayed on her even as he waved the dogs

outside, then he turned to face her fully and enjoy a view that far exceeded anything outside. Many nights he'd watched her sleep, her face relaxed, her stubborn chin softened a bit. Her long lashes brushed her sun-kissed cheeks. His body went hard all over again, his jeans more and more uncomfortable. He needed to get himself under control before she woke.

Padding barefoot across the room, he quietly put together the coffeepot. A crystal cake plate and cover displayed a selection of pastries big enough to feed them twice over. He grabbed a bear claw, wishing his other hunger was as easy to satisfy.

As the coffee gurgled the scent of java into the air, he felt the weight of eyes studying him. He already knew. Johanna. The connection that threatened to drive him mad was alive and well.

He pulled two stoneware mugs off the hooks under the cabinets. "Sorry I woke you."

A rustle from the sofa sounded, and her reflection came to life in the window pane over the sink.

"It's okay. I was just catnapping anyway." Johanna stretched her arms over her head. "It was tough to sleep after we argued."

"That wasn't an argument. I consider that a very revealing discussion we should have had a long time ago." He poured coffee into both mugs. Black. They both drank it the same way, strong and undiluted by sugar or cream. The only thing it seemed they still had in common. He picked up both and walked toward her.

"What would talking about my insecurities have changed?" Her bare toes curled against the rustic braid rug. "Do you think our breakup would have hurt any less? I can't imagine how."

"True enough." He passed her a mug, wishing he could find a way to be with her without tearing them both apart. "Truce?"

She took the mug, wrapping both hands around the mug, brushing his fingers. The ever-ready attraction crackled. He saw it echoed in her eyes, along with wariness.

"Truce," she repeated, sipping the coffee carefully. "Where to next?"

"Travel day, actually. I've got work to catch up on this morning." Not a total lie, since he always had work. "Then we'll fly out this afternoon to take Sterling to his new family in South Carolina."

"I'm almost afraid to ask who your grandmother lined up next. The president?"

"Just a former secretary of state."

She coughed a mouthful of coffee. "I was joking."

"I'm not." His grandmother moved in influential circles. He hadn't given a second thought to the families she had chosen. They were longtime friends. But he hadn't thought of how visiting these high-profile people would go over with Johanna. How many times had he tossed her into the middle of unfamiliar, perhaps even intimidating gatherings with no warning? Hell, he hadn't even given her any direction on how to pack, just offering to buy what she needed.

He'd hoped to use this time together to find peace for his grandmother—but also to find closure with Johanna. Okay, and also to have lots of sex with Johanna until they both were too exhausted to argue about the past. Then they could move on.

Clearly, his plan wasn't working out because he was falling into an old pattern of charging ahead and expecting her to follow. She didn't trust him and if she didn't trust him, there wasn't a chance in hell they could sleep together again.

He couldn't change the past, and he'd accepted they couldn't have a future together.

Although he could damn well do something about the present. For starters, he could share the details about their travel plans. But he would have to dig a lot deeper than that to fully regain her trust.

He sat beside her on the fat sectional sofa, trying to start right now, by including her in the plan for the week. "We'll be visiting the Landis-Renshaw family in Hilton Head. They've vacationed at the ranch before. As a matter of fact, they rented the whole place once for a family reunion."

"That would be quite a who's who of family reunions."

And he hadn't even told her their third stop would be to meet with a deposed European king.

Johanna welcomed the bustle of their travel day to Hilton Head, South Carolina. Stone had arranged for accommodations in a pet-friendly beach cottage with plenty of space for the dogs to run. They would meet with the Landis-Renshaw family in the morning.

Other cottages dotted the shoreline, but with an exclusivity that brought privacy. One other couple and a small family played in the surf, but otherwise she and Stone were on their own. She'd sensed a change in him earlier as he'd shared his plans for the South Carolina portion of their trip. He was genuinely attempting to include her, rather than simply taking charge.

So far, the truce they'd declared had held, due in

large part to how he'd included her. That helped her relax, taking away a layer of tension she hadn't even realized existed. She'd been worrying about the unknown.

She sat cross-legged on the wooden deck, a dozen steps away from him. The dogs curled up around her and she checked over each of them, making sure they hadn't picked up ticks in Vermont or sand spurs from their run along the beach earlier. She finished with Pearl, the search more extensive given the cairn terrier's longer fur.

Stone walked out of the surf like Poseidon emerging from the depths of the ocean. Big. Powerful. The hazy glow of the ending day cast him in shadows, his dark hair even blacker slicked with water. She'd always known Stone the cowboy entranced her more than Stone the CEO.

But Stone nearly naked absolutely melted her.

She forced her attention back to Pearl to keep from drooling over Stone in swim trunks. Her skin prickled with awareness as he opened the porch gate and walked past her. She heard the rattle of ice as he poured a glass of sweet tea before he dropped into one of the Adirondack loungers.

"How was the water?" She released Pearl to play with the other two dogs on the fenced deck.

"Good, good." He set his glass aside. "Everything okay with the dogs?"

They sounded like any other couple catching up at the end of the day, except there was this aching tension between them. "They all checked out fine. Just a couple of sandspurs on Pearl. I trimmed their nails, and I'll want to bathe them all after they run on the beach again. Otherwise, they're all set to meet their new families."

He swung his feet around, elbows on his knees. "You're a nurturer. It's in your blood."

Her hands clenched into fists to resist the urge to sweep sand from the hair on his legs. "Are you trying to needle me with the nurturer comment?"

"I'm just stating a fact. You'll make a great mother someday."

The humid night air grew thicker, her chest constricting. "You're good with children. The natural way you held little T.J....I just don't understand you."

"I'm good with horses, too. That doesn't mean I'm supposed to be a jockey," he said wryly.

"I wasn't insinuating you should be a father. You've been honest about your feelings on that subject. It just took me a while to stop thinking I could change your mind." Hugging her knees, she studied him in the fading light.

"I've always tried to be careful that women didn't get the wrong idea about me and wedding bells...until you."

That should have meant something, but it only served to increase the ache. "You're a playboy married to your work." She exhaled hard. "I get that. Totally."

Stone went quiet again for so long she thought they might be returning to the silent truce again. Awkward and painful.

Then Stone stood, walking to the rail and staring out at the ocean. "My father."

Rising, she moved to stand beside him, wind pulling at the whispery cover-up over her bikini. "What do you mean?"

His father had been an off-limits topic for as long as she'd known him. Not even Mariah brought up the subject. Stone had always said that according to his mom, his paternity was a mystery. Was he opening up to her on a deeper level, including her in more than a few travel plans?

"I found out." His voice came out hoarse and a little harsh as he continued to look out at the foaming waves.

She rested a hand on his arm tentatively, not sure how he would react but unable to deny him some comfort during what had to be a difficult revelation. "I wish you would have told me."

"I've never told anyone."

"I was supposed to be more than just 'anyone' to you," she reminded him softly.

He glanced sideways at her. "Touché."

"Did you hire a private investigator?"

"Don't you think my grandmother already tried that hoping to find someone who actually wanted me around?"

His words snapped her upright in shock. "Your grandmother loves you."

"I know that. I do," he said with certainty. "But she'd already brought up her kids. She was supposed to be my grandmother. Not my parent."

"Did she tell you that?" She knew full well Mariah never would have said anything of the sort to Stone. Johanna just wanted to remind him of how very much his grandmother loved him.

"She didn't have to say it." He went silent for the length of two rolling waves crashing to the shore. "When I was eleven, I found the private detective's report of her search for my biological father."

"Of course she would want to know everything about you. Perhaps she was worried that he might try to take you away. Did you ever consider that?" When he didn't answer, she continued, "You said she didn't find him. So how did you locate him?"

"The report uncovered a wealth of data about my mother's activities then." His face went darker. "Suffice it to say, my mother led quite an active party life."

"That reflects on her." She squeezed his arm. "Not on you."

"I understand that." He braced his shoulders, his eyes cold with an anger Johanna knew wasn't directed at her. "I'm not a drug addict like my mother. And while I'm not a monk, I'm monogamous during a relationship. I am my own man. I control myself and my destiny."

She rubbed soothing circles along his arm. Even if this conversation wouldn't change things between them, she knew he needed to get these words out and for some reason she was the person he trusted most to tell.

She drew in a bracing breath of salty air before continuing, "How did you find out about your father?"

"My mother told me."

"That simple?"

"Apparently so. She was high at the time and to this day doesn't remember telling me." He pinched the bridge of his nose. "I was twenty-five when she let it slip about the man who fathered me—Dale Banks."

Johanna gasped in recognition. "*The* Dale Banks? The country music star?"

"My mom was a groupie back in the day." He shrugged. "She hooked up with him and here I am."

She studied his features with a new perspective. Wind whipped her hair over her face, and she scraped the locks aside. "You do look a little like him. I never noticed until now…."

"I needed more reassurance than a look-alike contest. So I confronted him."

"How did you get past his security guards?"

"I have influence of my own." He smiled darkly. "Remember the benefit concert we sponsored a few years back?"

She did the quick math and realized Stone would have been in his mid-twenties then. She couldn't imagine how difficult that meeting must have been. "You arranged that to speak with him?"

"I'm not above using philanthropy for my own good, as well."

"You don't need to be sarcastic to cover your emotions." She slid her hand to his back and tucked her body to his side as if it was the most natural thing in the world to share his burdens. And it was. She drew in the heat and salty scent of him, her senses starved after months without him. "That had to have been difficult for you, confronting him."

"I didn't. I got a DNA sample during dinner."

"What?" She looked up sharply, unable to believe she'd heard him correctly. "You tricked him?"

"Easier than forcing the matter with a conversation where he denied it and I had to prove him a liar."

He didn't fool her for a second with this blasé act.

"What did he say when you finally told him?"

"He doesn't know. Why should he? He slept with a woman he didn't know and didn't care enough to follow up."

"Stone!" She cupped his face and made him look at her. "Maybe he's changed. Perhaps he has regrets and would like to know you now."

"I don't need him in my life," he said in a cold tone that left no room for negotiation.

"Maybe *he* needs *you*," she suggested. "People are so much more important than money or fame."

"That's right. You grew up poor but loved," he said sarcastically.

Again, he didn't fool her. She patted his cheek just a touch harder than a love tap. "Don't be a jerk."

"Maybe I'm letting my real side show." He turned his face to kiss her palm, then nipped it gently.

She wouldn't let him divert her with sex. She slipped her hand back down to his shoulder. "How did we spend so much time together and never talk about these things?"

"You were right in saying I was holding back."

She couldn't believe he'd admitted it. "Why are you telling me now? And please be truthful."

"I'm not really sure." He snagged a strand of her hair and stroked the length with gentle pressure. "Maybe because there's nothing left to lose between us. You've already ditched me. Why bother working my ass off to impress you?"

"You were working to impress me?" She couldn't resist smiling.

"Clearly, I failed." He looped the lock around his finger until he cupped the back of her head.

"Not totally." She stepped closer, unable to resist the sizzle, especially not combined with the vulnerability he'd shown in sharing what he'd found out about his father. "I did agree to marry you."

She arched up on her toes and kissed him. How could she not? Her body ached to be with him. They were two consenting adults, alone together, attached to no one else and both so very aware of the price of being together.

His arms banded around her, thick, muscled arms that held her with such gentle power she leaned closer until her breasts pressed to the hard bare wall of his chest. His mouth tasted of the salty ocean and sweet tea, a heady combination for a woman already teetering on the edge of losing control.

She sketched along the hard planes of his back, still damp from his swim and perspiration. So many nights she'd lain awake yearning to be with him again and now those restless fantasies were coming to life. Being away from home gave her the freedom to act on those impulses.

Stone caressed down her back to her hips, molding her closer to him, his arousal pressing against her stomach.

"Johanna," he groaned against her mouth. "You're killing me here. If you want to stop, we need to put the brakes on this now. It's up to you what happens next. How are we going to handle this attraction that's tearing us both apart?"

She dipped her hands into his swim trunks. "We're going to sleep together again. Tonight."

Seven

Finally, he had Johanna back in his arms again, even if just for a night. Only a fool would pass up this chance, and he was not a fool.

Taking her face in his hands, he kissed her, fully, tongues meeting and inhibitions gone. A perfect fit, just like before. Familiar and new all at once—their time apart added an edge to the need.

He backed her into the cottage, their bare legs tangling as they walked, notching his desire higher and higher with each provocative brush of skin against skin. Her fingers linked behind his neck as she writhed against him in a lithe dance of desire denied for far too long.

Impatiently, he pushed open the door with such urgency it slammed against the wall. His hands slid low, cupping her bottom and lifting her over the threshold. Once inside the cottage, he set her down, the bamboo floor cool under his feet in contrast to the heat searing through him.

Their bathing suits offered thin barriers between them, but too much right now. He bunched her whispery cover up in his hands and swept it over her head. He'd seen her in her bikini earlier—had seen her in far less—but she still took his breath away. Her simple black two-piece called to his hands, triangles begging to be peeled away.

She smiled with a siren's gleam in her eyes. "This is usually the point where you drop your Stetson on my head."

"I left it on my suitcase. Not too many cowboy hats on the beach while a guy's riding a wave."

"That's a damn shame." She traced the rope tattoo around his biceps, which ended in a lasso loop.

He and his cousins had gotten tattoos together when the twins had turned eighteen. He'd been twenty-one. Johanna had wanted to go with them. He'd forgotten that until just now. She'd wanted to get paw print tattoos on her ankle, but he'd known her parents wouldn't approve.

Tracing the length of her collarbone, he lifted the diamond horseshoe necklace she wore all the time now. "I would drape you in gems, design entire lines of jewelry dedicated to your beauty."

"Who knew you were poetic?"

"You inspire me."

She stroked up his arms. "I'm just as happy with wildflowers and bluebonnets. That day we made love in the open and you covered me in petals is one of my all-time favorite memories."

"Another reason you're special. I never have to wonder with you. I know you're here—or not here—based on me. It has nothing to do with my family or our money." He plucked the strings behind her neck. The top fell away, revealing her breasts, pert and a perfect fit in his palms.

"You're a savvy man," she gasped, her nipples beading against his hands, either from his touch or the cool swoosh of the air conditioner. "I imagine you see through the sycophants right away."

"That discernment came from practice." He thumbed along her taut peaks, teasing them tighter until she swayed ever so slightly.

She covered his hands with hers. "You shouldn't have to wonder about people that way. Thinking of you wondering, learning from practice—that makes me so sad."

"I definitely don't want you sad right now—or ever." He hooked his thumbs in the strings along her hips and snapped them before the thought formed in his mind.

Her swimsuit bottom fell away.

She kicked aside the scrap of fabric. "If I were the sort of woman who wanted to be draped only in jewels, what would you design for me?"

"Ah, now you're talking." He let his imagination take flight. "I've always liked yellow diamonds for you. I can see long earrings that trail in a sleek, thin cascade to your shoulders." He skimmed each spot with a kiss. "Each piece would echo the golden lines of your beautiful body. And a long, gold rope chain with a pendant that trails right…here…between…"

His mouth landed along the inside of one curve, then the other. Her breath hitched, her fingers twisting in the band of his swim trunks. Tugging at the elastic, she peeled the damp suit down and off into a pile around his feet.

He stepped out and then swept her up against his chest. "And since the jewelry would be for our eyes only, I dream of you in more erotic designs, as well."

"Oh, really?" She looped her arms around his neck. "I can't decide whether to be nervous or intrigued."

One step at a time, he carried her closer to the white

iron bed with a view of the water. "A thicker rope chain would circle low on your waist, resting on your hips."

"Ah, like a lasso." She thumbed his tattoo. "That works both ways, you know. I could pull you to me, especially perfect if you wore chaps and nothing more."

He arched an eyebrow. "Not very businesslike."

"We're not in the boardroom."

"True." He tossed her onto the mattress.

She landed with an enticing bounce that made all the right parts jiggle just a hint. She stretched out along the puffy quilt, her creamy shoulders propped up by a pile of seashell-patterned pillows.

Part of him wanted to take in the sight of her for hours on end, and another more urgent part of him couldn't delay any longer. He kneeled on the edge of the bed and crawled up over her, tasting his way up her bared flesh, along her stomach, teasing the diamond belly button ring with his teeth. Higher still, he took her breast in his mouth, rolling the nipple with his tongue until her needy sighs begged him for more, faster, sooner.

He glanced up to see her head thrown back, pushing into the pillows. From the flush blooming over her skin he knew she was close to coming apart. He understood the urgent sensation well and slid the rest of the way up to take her lips, his erection nudging against the slick core of her. Ready. For him. Just as he was ready for her, only her, always her.

With a hoarse growl, he thrust deep inside her.

Gasping, she grabbed his shoulders. "Stone, wait." She gripped harder, her fingernails digging into his flesh. "What about protection?"

He arched back to look into her eyes. "Aren't you on the pill?"

"Not anymore," she said. "Once we broke up and it was clear we weren't going to reconcile, I stopped taking it."

She'd thought about reconciling with him? For how long? How many opportunities had he missed to get her back only to lose her because of stubborn pride?

Have her back?

Wasn't this just about sex now?

All thoughts too weighty for him to consider with his brain muddled from being buried to the hilt inside her again.

He hadn't packed condoms…. And if they discussed this much further it was going to lead to a serious mood buster of a conversation. He rolled off her with a groan of frustration.

Johanna sat up with a gasp. "Wait." She snapped her fingers. "I saw some in the honeymooners' welcome basket on the bedside table."

Crisis averted. Thank heavens the staff had assumed they would need the romance special basket. He stayed on his side while Johanna raced into the living area, and yes, he enjoyed the hell out of the view. He'd dreamed of her, but fantasies couldn't come close to the reality of being here with her.

The sound of rustling carried from the next room before she returned. Grinning, she held a condom in one hand and a plump pear in the other. She sank her teeth into the fruit and tossed him the square packet. He snatched it out of midair then grabbed her wrist to tug her back into bed with him.

Laughing, she settled on top of him and pressed the

pear against his mouth. He took a bite, then set the fruit aside to have her. Johanna. His again.

He flipped her onto her back and thrust inside her. Gasping, she closed her eyes and welcomed him with a roll of her hips. Her legs wrapped around him, her heels digging in and urging him deeper, faster, leaving no room for misunderstanding. She wanted him, too, with the same hungry edge. He kissed her hard and insistent, the taste of pear mingling with the sweet warmth of her.

He knew her body as well as he knew his own. He'd made a point of learning each sensitive spot and how to tease her pleasure higher. And she'd done the same for him.

Touch for touch, they moved in synch with each other. Her hands roved a restless path until perspiration dotted his forehead in spite of the ocean breeze gusting through the window.

Wind chimes sang louder and louder as if kicked up by a spring storm. He whispered in her ear about husky fantasies built during nights apart, silver links binding them together, jewels hidden and found. Her panting replies—her yes, yes, yes riding each gasp— stoked the fire in him higher until his whole body felt like molten metal in a flame.

And just when he thought he couldn't hold out any longer before the heat consumed them both, Johanna flew apart in his arms. Her cries of completion rolled free, as uninhibited and natural as the woman in his arms. The sweet clamp of her body pulsing around him sent him over the edge with her.

As wave after wave crashed over him, he held her closer, absorbing her aftershocks as he slowly came back down to earth again. His arms gave way, and he rolled to his side, taking her with him.

With the wind kicking up a humid breeze and rain pattering outside, he willed his galloping heartbeat to return to normal. Except his hammering pulse wasn't cooperating. With each slug against his ribs, he knew.

He couldn't give Johanna up again, but there wasn't a chance in hell she would stay with him if she knew the worst of what he'd held back, the reason he absolutely could not fulfill her dreams and become the father of her children.

Johanna woke up to an empty bed.

She stretched under the Egyptian cotton sheets, the scent of lovemaking mingling with the ocean air blowing in through the window. Barks also echoed from outside along with the rumbling bass of Stone's voice shouting a ramble of "fetch" and "good girl."

The sun climbing high into the sky told her she'd slept in, not surprising since they'd made up for lost time throughout the night. In bed, in the shower, moving into the kitchen for food, then making love against the counter.

Her body carried the delicious ache of total satiation. Although she knew the moment she saw Stone, she would want him all over again, and she couldn't help but want to look her best. She shoved her hands through her tangled hair, which must be a complete mess since she'd gone to sleep with it still damp.

A quick glance at the clock had her rolling to her feet and racing to the bathroom. A fast washup later, she wrapped her hair and body in fluffy towels and opened the closet.

The packed full closet?

She stared at all the clothes that hadn't been there the night before. Tags showed they were all new and in her size. Stone had been busy. He'd ordered her a whole new wardrobe for the rest of their trip. He'd heard what she said about feeling uneasy and in his own way he was trying to ease that worry for her.

The barking dogs gave her only a moment's warning before Stone walked into the bedroom. So much for dressing up. She secured the towel around her and tugged the other off her head, shaking her hair free.

She skimmed her fingers along the rack of clothes. "You didn't have to do this, but thank you."

"Glad you're happy." He captured her hand and pulled her close. "And just so we're clear, it doesn't matter to me what you're wearing. In my eyes you're magnificent."

"Thank you." She arched up for a kiss. "You're one good cowboy, Stone."

"I'm trying, lady, I'm trying." He kissed her good-morning thoroughly before easing back. "I did hear what you said about going to formal functions before, and it's killing me to think you ever felt uncomfortable."

"I know a person's worth doesn't have anything to do with their bank balance."

"Damn straight." He dropped to sit on the foot of the bed, pulling her into his lap. "I imagine that's part of my grandmother's plan here, too, giving me a reality check when it comes to family values."

Her heart fluttered in her chest. He couldn't possibly be changing his stance on a family. Could he?

Afraid to wreck the moment by pushing, she changed the subject. "There's quite a range of clothes you've bought for me." She pointed to a rack with everything from jeans and slacks to sundresses and a couple of longer gowns. "Where else are we going?"

"My grandmother has a wide range of people lined up, even a couple of backups if someone doesn't work out."

She snagged an ice-blue lacy dress. "This looks fit for royalty."

"You're perceptive," he said with a grimace.

She rolled her eyes, certain she must have misunderstood. "Really? Royalty, in addition to a former secretary of state."

"Really."

She froze, realizing he was serious. "All right," she exhaled, sagging back against his chest. "If Sterling is going to the political powerhouse couple, that leaves Pearl and Ruby. Which one's getting the tiara?"

"Ruby. Enrique Medina lost both of his Rhodesian ridgebacks this year to old age. He and my grandmother are friends. He's even the one who recommended contacting General Renshaw about Sterling."

Royalty. Honest-to-God royalty. Nothing would surprise her about this family again. "What about Pearl? Is she going to the Pope?"

Stone snorted on a laugh. "I'm sure he's one of Gran's backups." He kissed her nose. "Seriously, though, I don't know as much about the last family other than that they live on a ranch in Montana."

"Are the formal gowns for the jewelers' convention that you mentioned?" Her stomach gripped at the thought. Even with the fancy clothes, she was still a farm girl who felt most at ease in her jeans, with braided hair and a horse.

"I canceled that. The variety of dresses are so we can go out to dinner somewhere nice. Just the two of us, to thank you for coming along this week to ease my grandmother's mind. Regardless of where we go from here, I will always be grateful for all you've done for Gran."

She couldn't help but be surprised again over how he was revealing more to her on this trip than she'd ever understood about him before. Had he suffered as much from their time apart? Or had confronting mortality with his grandmother's illness brought down some walls? Either way, she couldn't help but be drawn in by this man.

He tipped her chin for another kiss, one that couldn't go any further with the day slipping away, but God, she was tempted. Because she couldn't help but think these changes were too good to be true.

An hour later, Stone opened the hatch on their rental SUV to load up the dogs for their drive over to the Landis-Renshaw compound. Ruby loped into the back and he lifted scruffy little Pearl in, as well, a mesh barrier keeping them from taking over the front seat. He'd stowed their luggage in a cartop carrier. They looked like a regular family on vacation.

He rubbed the kink in his neck from lack of sleep, but he wouldn't change a moment of their night together.

The waves glistened under the power of the noonday sun and he wished they could just blow off his grandmother's plan and stay at the cottage for the rest of the week. He and Johanna had connected, just like in the past, and he was working hard to reassure her. Maybe he was deluding himself into hoping she could overlook the bigger issues if he corrected some other problems in their relationship.

To what end?

Did he really expect they would ride off into the sunset together? He had to be honest with himself and admit he wanted her back in his life on a permanent basis. But being equally honest, he wasn't sure that was possible no matter how many closets full of comfy clothes and easygoing outings he came up with.

The beach cottage door opened, and Johanna stepped out with Sterling cradled in her arms. She'd chosen a simple flowery dress, loose and classic. But she looked good in everything she wore. His assistant had ordered everything and assured him the task would be easy. Johanna had pulled her hair back in a jeweled clasp—a Diamonds in the Rough piece. And of course she wore his grandmother's horseshoe charm.

He struggled to resist the urge to scoop her up, carry her back inside and peel the dress off her. Instead, he held out his arms. "I'll take Sterling."

She shook her head, her ponytail sweeping along her spine the way his hands ached to do. "I'll hold him. I'm feeling sentimental about saying goodbye to him. I keep thinking about the day your grandmother got him as a puppy."

He closed the back hatch and walked around to open her door. "I always think of you as being there for the horses. I forget sometimes that caring for the dogs falls under your job description, as well." He leaned in the open door. "It will be tough for you to say goodbye to them, too."

"I don't have pets of my own...so yes." She stroked the Chihuahua-dachshund mix. "I have become at-

tached. But your grandmother is wise to make sure
they're placed. Too many animals end up at shelters
when their owners pass away or go into nursing homes."

"We would have taken them all for her. She has to
know that." Not a chance in hell would he have dumped
Gran's pets at the shelter. He closed the door, perhaps a
bit more forcefully than he'd intended, but the reminder
of a world without Mariah cast clouds over his day.

He walked around the hood and took his place behind the wheel. He swept off his Stetson and dropped
it on the console between them. Starting the car, he
pulled his focus back in tight before he landed them
nose first in a sand dune. Navigating the beach traffic
was tough enough.

Johanna's hand fell to rest on his arm as he passed a
slow-moving RV. "Clearly, Mariah has a plan in mind
for them, and for your future, too. Never doubt for a
second that she loves you."

He glanced at her. "She loves you, too, you know."

"Thank you—" she smiled "—but it's not the same.
I'm not family."

"I'm not so sure." His hands gripped the wheel
tighter, settling into their lane along the ocean side
road. "She was mad as hell with me when we broke up."

"Why was she angry with you?" Johanna sat up
straighter. "I was the one who ended our engagement.
I made that abundantly clear to everyone."

Had she made the breakup public to spare him blow-
back from his family? He'd been so angry at her then,
he hadn't given thought to the fact that a public breakup
actually cast him in a more sympathetic light. He'd been
too caught up in his anger—and hurt. "Gran said I had

to have done something wrong to make you give back the engagement ring. And she was right."

The breakup had been his fault, and nothing significant had changed. He still didn't want children, and watching her cradle the dog, he couldn't miss her deep-seated urge to nurture.

He felt like a first-class ass.

Johanna adjusted the silver collar around Sterling's neck. "I'm sorry if I caused a wedge between the two of you."

"You have nothing to apologize for," he insisted, steering onto a bridge that would take them to their barrier island destination. "I'm an adult. My relationships are my own problem."

"She's trying to matchmake, sending us on this trip together." Johanna traced the top of his hat resting between them.

No kidding. "I'm sure that was a part of her plan, no matter what she said, but the rest is still true." Miles of marshy sea grass bowed as they drove deeper into the exclusive beach property of Hilton Head, the South's answer to Martha's Vineyard. "She doesn't trust me to see to the dogs, and she's right. I would have screwed it up."

"I seriously doubt that," Johanna said with a confidence he didn't feel when it came to this subject.

"I wouldn't have been as thorough as you've been." He'd been impressed and surprised during the meet and greet with the Donavans. "I wouldn't have even thought of half the things you've done to make sure Gem's in the right home and that the transition goes smoothly for her."

"Gem's going to miss your grandmother." She swept

a hand under her eyes and he realized she'd teared up. "There will be grieving on his part as well."

"Are you trying to make me just skip the rest of this trip and take the dogs home with us? Because I'm about five seconds away from doing that," he half joked. "In fact, much more of this and I'll even snatch Gem back."

She responded with a watery laugh. "Don't you dare. The Donavans are a fantastic family for Gem, as Mariah clearly already knew." She reached into her bag and pulled out dog treats. She passed two over the mesh to Pearl and Ruby, before offering another to Sterling. "They're not cutie pie little puppies anymore, and placing an adult dog can be difficult. And we definitely don't want someone taking in the dogs in hopes of gaining favor with your grandmother."

Protectiveness pumped through him. "I wouldn't let that happen."

"Of course not. You're a good man."

"Such a good man my grandmother has to test me and you dumped me flat on my ass," he said wryly.

She scooted closer, slipping her hand to the back of his neck. "I miss the happy times between us. Last night was…incredible."

What an odd time to realize she was "soothing" him the same way she soothed Sterling, using her dog whisperer ways on him. "So you do acknowledge it wasn't all bad between us."

"Of course it wasn't all bad," she said incredulously.

"Specifics." He might as well use this time to get whatever edge he could.

"Why?" Suspicion laced her voice. "What purpose will it serve?"

"Call it a healing exercise." And the hope of figuring out a way to have more with her tomorrow.

"Okay, uh…" Her hand fell back to the dog in her lap. "I appreciate the way you support my work. Like the time I'd already pulled extra hours on my shift, but the call came from a shelter in South Texas in need of extra veterinary help for neglected horses seized by animal control. You drove through the night so I could sleep before working." Her mouth tipped in a smile, her eyes taking on a faraway look. "Then you didn't sleep. You rolled up your sleeves and helped."

He had to haul his gaze away from the beauty of her smile before he rear-ended the car in front of them. "We accomplished a lot of good together that day."

"We did. And I know it was you who encouraged your grandmother to help sponsor this year's big charity event to help save the wild mustangs."

He shrugged, her praise making him itchy. "We needed a tax write-off."

"You're not fooling me." She swatted his arm.

He searched for the right words. "My family has worked hard and been very lucky. We're in a position to do good."

"Not everyone makes the same choices as your family. I don't even know that I'd fully thought about it in such concrete terms until now. Your grandmother instilled solid values in all of you."

"Very diplomatic of you not to mention what my mom or Amie and Alex's parents could have shared." Diplomatic and astute.

"I'm sorry that your mother couldn't be a true parent for you."

"Don't be." The warmth of the day chilled for him.

"She broke Gran's heart. And Uncle Garnet wasn't much better, but at least he tried to build a normal family life. He went to work every day even if he wasn't particularly ambitious." Or willing to stand up to his overly ambitious wife. "Gran always said she babied him and she wanted to be sure she didn't make the same mistake with us."

"Your aunt Bayleigh was ambitious enough for the both of them." She shuddered dramatically.

"True enough." There was no denying the obvious. "She pushed the twins for as far back as I can remember. Although I gotta confess, even their flawed family looked mighty damn enticing to me as a kid."

"You wanted to live with them."

She sounded surprised, which made him realize yet again how little of himself he'd shared with the woman who was supposed to have been the most important person in his life. If he wanted even a chance at being with her again, he had to give what he could this time.

"I did want to be their kid," he admitted. "Gran even asked them once if they would be interested in guardianship of me, but their plate was full."

She gasped. "That had to be so painful to hear."

To this day, he was glad no one had seen him listening in. He couldn't have taken the humiliation of someone stumbling on him crying. Looking back, he realized he must have only been in elementary school, but the tears had felt less than manly on a day when he already felt like a flawed kid no one wanted.

"It worked out for the best." He found himself still minimizing the pain of that experience. "Gran was a great parental figure. And my mother, well, she was a helluva lot of fun during her sober stints."

The words came out more bitterly than he'd intended. Thank God, they were pulling up to the security gate outside the Landis-Renshaw compound because he'd had about as much "sharing time" as he could take for one day. Much more of this and he would start pouring out stories about being a crack baby, who still cringed at the thought of all the developmental psychologists he'd visited before he'd even started first grade.

He was managing fine now, damn it, and the past could stay in the past.

The wrought-iron security gates loomed in front of them, cameras peeking out of the climbing ivy. He rolled down his window and passed over his identification to a guard posted in his little glass booth with monitors.

The guard nodded silently, passed the ID back, and the gates swung open. Now he just had to figure out how to say goodbye to another family pet and pretend it didn't matter that the only family he'd known would soon fall apart when his grandmother died. She'd been his strength and his sanity. She'd literally saved his life as a baby. She was a strong woman, like Johanna.

As he watched Johanna cuddle the dog in her lap, he realized he hadn't taken this dog placement trip seriously, which was wrong of him. He'd just followed Johanna's lead in shuffling his grandmother's pets to new families, not thinking overlong about the loss, just going through the motions. His grandmother, Johanna—the dogs—all deserved better than that from him.

For the first time he considered that perhaps his grandmother hadn't been matchmaking after all. Maybe she had been trying to help him understand why Johanna was better off without him.

Eight

Settled deep in the front seat of the SUV, Johanna wrapped her arms around the dachshund mix in her lap and wondered how she'd gotten drawn back into a whirlwind of emotions for Stone so quickly.

At least once they arrived, she had the next few hours with people around to give her time to regain her footing before they were in a hotel together or some other romantic setting on this trip designed to tamper with her very sanity. She had time to build boundaries to protect her heart until she could figure out where they were going as a couple. Was this just sex for the week or were they going to try for more again? If so, they still had the same disagreements looming as before.

She hugged the dog closer as she looked through the window to take everything in. Could this day be any more convoluted? She was seconds away from meeting a political powerhouse couple. The general was reputed to be on the short list for the next secretary of defense. Ginger was now an ambassador and former secretary of state. Her oldest son was a senator. Who wouldn't be nervous?

Stone, apparently.

He steered the car smoothly, but his mind was obviously somewhere else. "I never did know how Sterling ended up in my grandmother's pack."

His comment surprised her.

"One of her employees was older and developed Alzheimer's. The retirement home the woman's family chose didn't allow animals."

"That's really rough. How did I not know that story?" His forehead furrowed as he steered the SUV up the winding path through beach foliage to the main house. "I wish my grandmother would have trusted me more to see to the animals after she's gone so she could have the comfort of them now when she needs them most."

Johanna stayed silent. She agreed 100 percent but saying as much wouldn't change anything. The situation truly was a tough one. "It's sad Sterling should lose his owner twice."

"Life is rarely about what's fair," he said darkly before sliding the car into Park alongside the house.

He grabbed his hat and was out of the car before she could think of an answer. What was going on inside his head? This man never ceased to confuse her.

While she secured Sterling's leash, she studied the grounds to get her bearings before she stepped out of the car. The beach compound was grander than the rustic Hidden Gem Ranch and more expansive than the scaled-back Donavan spread. She'd seen photos from a *Good Housekeeping* feature when she'd searched the internet for more details on the Landis and Renshaw families, who had joined when the widowed Ginger Landis married the widower General Hank Renshaw. But no magazine article could have prepared her for the breathtaking view as Johanna stared through the windshield. The homes were situated on prime oceanfront property. The main house was a sprawling white three-story overlooking the Atlantic, where a couple walked along the low-crashing waves. A lengthy set of stairs stretched upward to the second-story wraparound porch that housed the double door entrance.

Latticework shielded most of the first floor, which appeared to be a large entertainment area, a perfect use of space for a home built on stilts to protect against tidal floods from hurricanes. The attached garage had more doors than an apartment complex.

A carriage house and the Atlantic shore were in front of them. And two cottages were tucked to the sides around an organically shaped pool. The chlorinated waters of the hot tub at the base churned a glistening swirl in the sunlight, adults and kids splashing.

It was a paradise designed for a big family to gather in privacy. The matriarch and patriarch of the family—Ginger and the general—appeared on the balcony porch looking like any other grandparents vacationing with their family. Relatives of all ages poured from the guest quarters. Three other dogs sprinted ahead. Not quite the careful, structured meet and greet that worked best, but clearly this home was about organized chaos.

She stepped out of the car, setting Sterling on the sandy ground while she held tight to the leash. The family tableaus played out in full volume now. She could hear a little girl squealing with laughter while her dad taught her to swim in the pool. A mom held a snoozing infant on her lap while she splash, splash, splashed a toe in the water. Voices mingled from a mother's lullaby to a couple planning a date night since grandparents could babysit.

Johanna saw her own past in the times her parents

had taken her swimming in a pond and saw the future she wanted for herself, but couldn't see how Stone would fit into it. She was killing herself, seeing all these happy families while was stuck in a dead-end relationship with a man who would never open up.

All luxury aside, this kind of togetherness was what she'd hoped to build for herself one day. Those dreams hadn't changed. Which meant she'd landed herself right back into the middle of a heartache all over again.

Stone sat at a poolside table with Ginger and Hank Renshaw, pouring over their adoption paperwork. If anyone had told him a week ago that he would be grilling them to be sure Sterling would be a happy fit for their family, Stone would have said that person was nuts.

Yet here he was, quizzing them and watching the way they handled his grandmother's dog— Correction. *Their* dog now. Sterling was curled up in Ginger's lap, looking like a little prince, completely unfazed by the mayhem of children cannonballing into the deep end while a volleyball game took place on the beach.

Stone nodded somberly, pulling his hat off and setting it aside. "It's important that Sterling get along with children."

"Amen," the general agreed, having stayed silent for the most part, a laid-back gramps in khaki shorts and a polo shirt. "We have double digits in grandkids. Christmases are particularly chaotic."

This wasn't chaos? Stone felt the weight of Johanna's eyes on him, the confusion in her gaze. He gave her a reassuring smile, and she warily smiled back, which too quickly had his mind winging back to thoughts of last night, of how damn much he enjoyed making her smile…and sigh.

He cleared his throat, and his thoughts, turning his focus back to the older couple who'd clearly found a second chance at romance.

Ginger touched her husband's arm, the former secretary of state completely poised in spite of the breeze pulling at her graying hair and loose beach dress. "Hank, we should have them test out the Rottweiler—Ruby—while they're here, as well, since he will be part of the family, sort of, by going to Jonah's father-in-law."

Ginger's youngest son had married a princess, no less. Stone looked out at the beach where Ruby splashed in the waves with another dog and a trio of preteens. "So far so good, I would say."

Ginger nodded, patting the cairn terrier in Johanna's lap. "I just wish we could take that precious Pearl, too. She's like a little Toto from *The Wizard of Oz*. The grandkids would love her and it would be wonderful to keep them together. But we know our limits."

Johanna set her glass of sweet tea back on the table. "We're going to be sure Pearl is well taken care of. Just knowing that Sterling is happy is a load off all our minds, especially for Mrs. McNair." She glanced sympathetically at Stone before looking back at Ginger. "Thank you."

The family matriarch twisted a diamond earring in a nervous fidget, genuine concern in her eyes. "I'm terribly sorry about Mariah…. There are no words at a time like this."

"Thank you, ma'am." Stone nodded tightly, emotion squeezing his chest in a tight fist. "You're offering exactly the kind of help my grandmother needs. Right, Johanna?"

He glanced at her, finding her gaze locked on a mother, father and toddler splashing through the surf together. The look of longing in her eyes slashed straight through him.

Johanna stood up quickly. "We brought a little gift, as a thank-you from Diamonds in the Rough. I'll just get it out of the car."

As he watched her race away he realized how their night together had messed with both of them. Last night had been different from their other times together, and his emotions were in revolt. He was starting to accept it wasn't totally because of his grandmother. His confusion had more to do with Johanna than he'd realized.

Strange how they'd swapped roles here, but he appreciated her interjecting. Talk of his grandmother and seeing this picture-perfect family echoed what he'd already begun to accept. Johanna was right to want this for herself. She shouldn't compromise for him.

On the plane headed for Montana for Pearl's meeting, Johanna struggled to figure out the shift in Stone this afternoon. She thought they'd reached a truce whereby they would indulge in no-strings sex for the week and deal with the fallout later. Yet, something had already changed for him.

And she had to confess, she didn't feel carefree about things, either. Watching the huge Landis-Renshaw family hurt. She couldn't lie about that.

The plane powered through the bumpy night sky and even though she knew where they were going literally, figuratively, she was now totally adrift.

She studied Stone sitting on the sofa with a sketch pad, his forearm flexing as he drew. Pearl slept on a cushion beside him, her head resting on his thigh. He was so damn enticing, he took her breath away.

"What happens now?" Johanna asked.

He glanced up. "Well, in about two more hours, we should land in—"

"That's not what I meant." Her hand fell to Ruby's head as the Rottweiler slept at her feet. Johanna would kennel them for landing or if the turbulence worsened, but for now she wanted to make the most out of the remaining time with the dogs before they went to their new homes. "Why are you avoiding talking to me? I really don't want to think that now that you've gotten lucky we're through."

His eyebrows shot upward. "You have a mighty jaded view of mankind."

"You haven't said anything to change my mind tonight," she pushed.

Eyes narrowed, he set aside his sketch pad and rolled his broad shoulders to stretch out a kink. "Who gave you such a bad impression of men, and why didn't I pick up on this when we were together before?"

"Maybe because I always gave you the answers you wanted to hear." She was realizing she had to accept some responsibility for their breakup and quit blaming him for everything.

"And I accepted them rather than pressing," he conceded, bracing his feet through another brief patch of turbulence.

"There's no great mystery to be solved." She shrugged. The muted cabin lights, with only a reading lamp over Stone, cast intriguing shadows along his rugged face. "My parents were great. My father was a good man. But for some reason, the men I chose to date always let me down. One wanted me to give up vet tech school to follow him right away, no waiting—"

"That was Dylan—"

"Yeah," she said, surprised that Stone remembered. He'd been intensely into making his mark at the company, so much so she'd decided she needed to get over her crush. She'd been living in an efficiency apartment, training to be a vet tech. It had seemed time to move forward with her life. "He couldn't even wait six more months for me to finish."

"Then he didn't deserve you."

"Damn right." She knew that now, and even then she'd felt a hint of relief since she didn't ever want to leave Fort Worth. "And the next guy I dated when I moved back to the ranch after school—"

"Langdon."

"You have a good memory." A part of her had wanted him to notice she'd grown up, had wanted him to see her as a woman rather than the pigtailed kid trailing around in the stables. Hindsight, that had been incredibly unfair to Langdon.

"When it comes to you? Yes, I have a very good memory."

"Langdon was the jealous type." And there had been reason for him to be jealous, but that still didn't excuse him going borderline stalker about it. "No need to say more."

"I disagree," he said darkly.

"Don't get caveman on me. You don't need to hunt him down. He didn't hurt me." She stared out into the murky sky for a moment before continuing, "But a look in his eyes made me uncomfortable. I could go on about the other guys in my life, but I just kept picking losers."

"Ouch," he snapped back with a laugh, scrubbing a hand along his five o'clock shadow. "That stings since I'm on that list of exes."

"One of my exes accused me of entering relationships destined to fail because I was secretly pining for you." The words fell out before she could recall them, but then, what did she have to lose at this point?

"Was that true?"

"You know I always had a crush on you." The crush had been so much easier than this.

"Crushing and loving are very different."

Her stomach lurched and it had nothing to do with the bump, bump of the plane over another air pocket. "I did love you when we got engaged."

"Past tense...." He rubbed his neck, and her fingers clenched at the memory of the warmth of his skin. "I'm still getting used to that. What about now?"

"I honestly don't know, and the way you're sitting over there all detached makes it even tougher to figure out what I'm feeling."

He stood, and her mouth went dry the way it always did when he walked her way. But instead of scooping her up, he simply moved into a large leather chair across from her. "When we were together at the beach, none of that was pretend. You can trust what we felt."

"It was real, but we're still learning things weren't as perfect as we thought they were the day we got engaged. It will take us both some time to trust anyone again."

His jaw flexed with tension. "The thought of you getting over me enough to be with someone else is not a heartening thought."

"Why do you naturally assume that the someone I should be with would have to be another person?" She wanted to grab him by the shoulders and shake him. What the hell was going on? He'd made it clear he didn't want to break up when she'd walked, and now that she was reaching out, he'd put up a wall between them. "Even after what we shared last night?"

"Is this really a discussion we should be having now?"

"If not now, when?"

Turbulence jostled the plane again, harder this time and Ruby scrambled for steady footing.

Stone rose quickly, no doubt welcoming the chance to avoid the tough conversation. "We should crate the dogs now."

Sighing, Johanna rose, too, walking to the sofa to pick up Pearl. The pup sat on top of the sketch pad, head tipped with total attitude, one ear up, one down. Johanna gathered the scruffy rascal and uncovered Stone's sketch pad.

A gasp hitched in her throat as she looked down at a page filled with all the fantasy jewelry pieces he'd described wanting to create just for her, and in the middle of it all, a drawing of her sitting in a field of bluebonnets with Pearl beside her. The attention to detail was mind-blowing, even down to the weave of her French braid.

The whole time she'd thought he was pushing her away, he'd been focused completely on her.

Stone secured the latch on Ruby's crate. The Rottweiler stared back with droopy sad eyes as she curled up on her fluffy green dog bed. He plucked a dog biscuit from the bin beside the crates and passed a treat through. This week with Johanna was getting more and more complicated and he didn't know how to return to the connection they'd enjoyed while staying at the beach.

She knelt beside him, sliding Pearl into the smaller crate with a pink doggie bed and a couple of chew toys. Just as she locked the pup in, the plane jostled again. And again. Johanna tumbled against him, knocking him back. He twisted fast to cushion her fall with his body.

Johanna stretched out on top of him. "Oh, my, that was something."

He tugged her loose ponytail. "I'm not right for you and you shouldn't settle."

"I know that, and yet here we are."

God, he knew he wasn't good enough for her and still he could already hear that voice in the back of his mind insisting he try to repair the damage that had been done in the past and clear away obstacles to their future.

She wriggled against him enticingly. "Do we have enough time to slip away into the back cabin before we land?"

He clamped a hand on her bottom, acknowledging that he was still unable to resist this woman. He couldn't envision a time he could ever keep her at arm's length. So yeah, he was a selfish bastard. "Keep moving like that and we won't need much time at all."

Laughing, she leaned down to kiss him. The turbulence dipped the plane, and they rolled, slamming against the dog crates.

The captain's voice rumbled over the intercom, announcing the need to return to their seats and buckle in until they cleared the turbulence.

Stone's low curse whispered between them before

he levered off her. He extended a hand to help her up while bracing his other palm along her back protectively to steady her as they returned to the sofa and dug out the seat belts. He took the sketch pad, flipped it closed fast and tossed it aside.

She clicked the lap belt and tugged the strap. "I felt much better for Ruby after hearing the Renshaws' feedback. Makes me hopeful that will work well, too. I wish we knew more about Pearl's family in Montana."

"Honestly, I'm surprised my grandmother isn't keeping Ruby, since that's the one dog she chose rather than adopting from someone else. I never thought to ask Gran about Ruby's history. She just said she got Ruby at a shelter, nothing more."

"Your grandmother seemed lonely after she retired from the board at Diamonds in the Rough. So I took her to the animal shelter. She chose a new friend. Ruby was a stray, no known history, but they took to each other right away."

"You're a good woman, Johanna. I've always known that, though." His hand fell on her knee.

"Don't try the übercharmer act on me." She leaned closer and tapped him on the chin.

"It's not an act," he denied even as he slid his hand under the hem of her dress, ideas flourishing for ways to please her in spite of the seat belt. "If I were just trying to charm you, I would compliment your beautiful face or your hot body...." He skimmed up the inside of her thigh, welcoming the distraction from more serious talk and concerns. If only he could lose himself in her infinitely.

"Which is all true, of course," he continued. "That's what reeled me into asking you out. But the good woman part?" He squeezed her thigh without moving any higher. "That's what kept me around. That's why I proposed. And ultimately, that's why you left me."

"What are you trying to accomplish?" There was anguish in her beautiful eyes, but a whisper of hope that spurred him on and crystalized his thoughts.

"It's a warning, I guess," he said somberly, sliding his hand from under her dress to take her fingers in his. "You are a good woman, and you deserve better than what I have to offer. But that isn't going to stop me from offering and asking again."

Her throat moved in a slow swallow. "Stone—"

"Shh." He pressed a finger to her lips. "I don't want you to answer yet. You should think. And just so you know, all I can think about is peeling your clothes away piece by piece, then making love to you in a field of bluebonnets."

"Are you really suggesting we just have sex and… drift?"

"If that means I get more time with you, then yes," he answered without hesitation. "There is no one else I'll be spending my life with. You were it, Johanna. My one shot at the whole happily-ever-after gig."

He cupped her face and drew her to him, easy to do as she leaned into him. Her fingers fluttered along his cheek, falling to rest on his shoulders. Her light touch stirred him every bit as much as her most bold caress.

Damn straight, there was no one for him other than Johanna. He deepened the kiss, her soft lips parting for him, inviting him in to taste, take and give. The warmth of her seeped into him, fanning the flames that never died. She was in his blood, now and always.

He tugged the band from her hair and combed his

fingers through the strands. The feel of her hair gliding along his hands was pure bliss, like the wind sliding over him when he rode on the open land. He played it out along her back and over her shoulders before stroking down her arms.

His hand returned to her knee and tunneled under her silky dress, along her even silkier thigh. His knuckles skimmed her satin panties, already hot from her arousal, and he ached to know what color she wore—

The plane's phone rang from beside the sofa, jarring him from the kiss and the moment. Who would call in the middle of the night? Only family and only with an emergency.

With more than a little regret, he ended the kiss and pulled away from Johanna, alarms already sounding in his mind. He angled past her to snag the phone and read the screen. He glanced at Johanna, apprehension filling his gut as his suspicion was confirmed.

"It's Amie." He frowned, thumbing the on button and activating the speakerphone. "Amie, what's up? You're on speaker. Johanna's here with me."

"Gran's in the hospital." His cousin's voice trembled, and Stone exchanged a quick glance with Johanna. "She had a seizure, Stone. It… It was…horrible. We had to call an ambulance."

Dread hit him like a boulder. "I'm on my way. I'll have the pilot turn around, and we'll be there in a few hours. Hold on, okay, kiddo?"

He vaguely registered Johanna's hand smoothing along his back.

Amie hiccupped on the other end of the line. "I'm sorry to be such a mess. It was just really frightening." The sound of her shaky breath reverberated on the crackly connection. "Alex and I can hold down the fort until you get here. The doctor says she's past the immediate danger, but…"

"I'm on my way," he repeated, pulling his focus in tight. He was the head of his family. He should be home overseeing the business and the family affairs for his grandmother, not playing games.

He owed his grandmother and Johanna better. From this point on, he was 100 percent in when it came to taking care of his family, and Johanna was going to be a member of his family.

Whatever it took.

Nine

Johanna's stomach dropped as the hospital elevator rose, taking them to Mariah.

Fear for Mariah and grief for Stone had tumbled and tangled inside her ever since the panicked call from Amie came through. And no matter how much she worried, there was nothing she could do to console Stone or make this better.

They should be bonded in the moment, leaning on each other while they were both scared and hurting, but instead she could see him drawing inward. Rather than letting anyone close, Stone took on the leader of the pack mentality that had kept him at the office late so many nights. Since he'd hung up the phone, he'd been in motion. He'd moved up front with the pilot to discuss rerouting the plane. A limo had met them at the airport driving them to the ranch to drop off the dogs and grab a quick shower.

Now, medical personnel on the fourth floor milled around the nurses' station watching over their patients through cameras and observation windows. His grandmother had plenty of watchful eyes but Stone had already started researching other hospitals and doctors without even consulting the rest of the family. God, she hoped there wouldn't be a major argument with Stone and his cousins.

The head nurse waved him through before returning to her charts. Stone had called ahead to confirm the minute morning visiting hours began. She didn't even want to consider the fact that they could have arrived too late.

Mariah looked pale and small under the stark white sheet, sleeping. Only the steady rise and fall of her chest and the monitors beeping and clicking offered any reassurance that she was still alive.

Stone swept off his hat, set it on the rolling tray and moved closer to his grandmother. His boots thudded softly against the tile floors.

Mariah's lashes fluttered upward, her eyes surprisingly clear and alert, thank heavens. "You're here." She reached out a thin hand, her skin almost translucent. "I told your cousins not to worry you. Which one called?"

"I'm not ratting anyone out," he teased softly.

Mariah laughed softly. "You three always did stick together." She looked past him and smiled at Johanna, lifting her other hand with the IV line taped down. "Dear girl, come closer. You can both do away with those gloom and doom looks on your faces."

Johanna stroked Mariah's wrist. "Of course we're worried. You would feel the same if our positions were reversed."

"True enough," Mariah conceded. "But I'm okay. It was only a case of dehydration. Nothing to do with the tumor. I let myself get run-down and just needed a little boost. It's my own fault, and I'm so sorry they scared you into coming home unnecessarily."

"Gran, you don't need to lie to me." Stone's forehead furrowed, his face bristly since he'd rushed his shower and skipped the shave. "I already know you had a seizure."

"Damn it, I told Amie and Alex not to worry you, and don't bother denying one of them told you," she groused with enough spunk that Johanna relaxed a hint. "I'm not going to die this week, so you two don't need to park by my bed and babysit me. You have work to do."

Stone dropped into the chair by her bed. "They knew how angry I would be once I found out no one bothered to call me. And believe me, I would have found out."

"You're just like me." She smiled fondly. "Tenacious."

"I'm just glad you're all right, Gran." He glanced across his grandmother at Johanna, the strain of the past few hours showing in the lines fanning from his sapphire-blue eyes. "We both are."

Mariah squeezed Johanna's hand. "Tell me about your trip so far. The pictures are wonderful but I want to hear what you think, Johanna."

Mariah was shifting topics deftly, ensuring Stone wouldn't have to battle through weightier emotions right now. Or was it Mariah who wasn't ready to face those feelings today? Johanna had never fully appreciated how alike the two of them really were. But for now, she gladly distracted both of them with talk of a safe subject.

"Well, Gem loves the wide-open space of the Donavans' home, and their home in Monte Carlo has a fenced area, as well. Sterling is enjoying his life as a pampered lapdog. You chose well for both of them."

Her eyelids fluttered closed for a moment before she

looked up at Stone and Johanna again with a mist of tears in her eyes. "Thank you, and I truly mean that."

"Gran." Stone leaned in. "Are you sure you want us to continue with the placements? You could keep Pearl and Ruby. Trust that we will take care of finding them new homes, if the time comes—" He swallowed hard, his Adam's apple making a slow trip down the strong column of his throat. "If the time comes you can't care for them anymore."

Johanna had to blink her eyes hard. God, maybe it was her who wasn't ready to face the big emotions in the room today. Mariah had become so dear to her. A role model. A friend.

"I'm absolutely certain that I want you to continue the plan." She smiled sadly. "I already can't give them the attention they need. Call me a micromanager if you will, but I need to know where they are and who they're with."

"Gran—" Stone's phone cut him short and he cursed softly. He pulled out the cell and checked the incoming call, before silencing the chimes and tucking the phone back in his pocket.

His grandmother touched his wrist. "Who is it? Your cousins?"

He shook his head. "It's from Montana. Probably something about Pearl. I'll take it later."

"No," Mariah said with surprising strength. "That's important business to me."

His cheeks puffed out with an exhale. "Okay, Gran. If that's what you want, but I'll be right back."

Phone to his ear, head ducked, he strode out, door swooshing closed behind him.

Mariah patted Johanna's hand. "Pull up a seat and talk to me, Johanna. How is it really going, dear?"

"What do you mean?" she asked evasively, looking away under the guise of tugging a chair over.

"No need to be coy," Mariah tsked. "Are you and Stone a couple again?"

Johanna dropped into a seat. "Wow, you really cut to the chase."

"I don't have time to dillydally around the subject." Mariah pushed the controls to raise the head of the mattress. "Even at half speed in this hospital bed, I can tell the chemistry is alive and well. I see the exchanged glances. You have to know I was hoping your trip together would fix things between you. Did my matchmaking work?"

The optimism in the woman's face was unmistakable. Johanna didn't want to give false hope, and she wasn't sure where things stood with Stone right now. "I wish I could tell you what you want to hear, but I honestly don't know."

"The fact that you didn't deny it outright gives me hope."

Johanna sagged back, rolling her eyes. "But no pressure, right?"

"You're more confident now than you were a year ago." She nodded approvingly. "That's a good thing. Your parents would be very proud of you."

She couldn't deny that Mariah's words of encouragement meant a great deal to her. "Thank you. I appreciate that, but please just focus on taking care of yourself. You're important to a lot of people."

"You've always been dear."

Johanna scrunched her nose. "You make me sound wimpy."

"I just told you I see your confidence and I meant that." Mariah studied her with perceptive eyes. "But there is a gentleness to you that my grandson needs in his life. It softens his harsher edges."

Johanna found herself growing defensive on his behalf. "Why is it that everyone assumes because his mother named him Stone he's hard-hearted?"

Mariah smiled. "And that's why you're perfect for him."

Stone ended his phone call the second he saw Amie and Alex entering the visitors' waiting room. The muted sounds from a mounted television broadcasting a talk show mingled with the soft conversations from a handful of other people in the waiting area. Fake plants and magazine racks were tucked into one corner. A coffeepot gurgled in the other.

He and his cousins had spent little time alone together since their grandmother's announcement. His gut twisted at the realization they would be meeting up in waiting rooms like this many more times in the coming months.

In light of that, any bickering between them felt like a waste of precious time. And the frustration with the Montana family that had changed their mind about Pearl? He would deal with that later.

He had Johanna's reassurance that there was nothing between her and Alex, and Stone couldn't blame his cousin. Johanna was an amazing woman.

Alex stuffed his hands in his jean pockets and rocked back on his boot heels. "You've seen Gran already?"

Stone nodded, tucking an arm around Amie, her shoulders too thin beneath her silk blouse. "She seems alert, just tired. Thank you for calling me."

Amie hugged him back quickly before stepping away. "Alex said not to bother you."

Alex shrugged. "I've got things under control here, so you can finish up your business with the dogs."

Stone held back the urge to chew out Alex for being an ass. Even his quiet cousin would have blown a gasket if left out of the loop on news about Mariah's health.

Torqued at Alex's attitude, Stone couldn't resist jabbing, "Wait until you're the one turning your life upside down to make her happy. And you know damn well you both will."

He glowered at his cousin until he was sure Alex understood he wouldn't have appreciated being left in the dark about Gran. Then, hoping to distract Amie, he asked, "Any idea from Gran about what test she has in mind for the two of you?"

Amie shuffled from high heel to high heel, gnawing her thumbnail. "She hasn't mentioned it, but you know there's no rushing Gran. She has a plan and a reason for everything she does." She looked at her hand as if only just realizing she was chewing her nails down to nothing. She tucked her fist behind her back. "Have you told your mother yet?"

"Why would I?" Stone retorted quickly. "If Gran wants to see her, she'll tell her."

Alex lifted a lazy eyebrow. "Have you ever considered we should overrule Gran? Not just on this, but on other issues, as well. You have to confess that this test thing to decide the future of a huge estate is more than a little half-baked."

Stone stared at Alex in surprise. His cousin was a man of few words, so a speech that long carried extra weight.

Amie crossed her arms tightly, a wrist full of delicate silver bangles jangling. "You can't be saying what I think. You can't intend to have Gran declared unfit to manage her affairs."

"I think we should consider it," Alex said somberly. "She even said she planned this test for you because she was afraid the tumor might affect her judgment. What if it's too late?"

Stone hated even considering it. But had he disregarded warning signs about his grandmother out of a selfish need to have Johanna back in his life? "This isn't a question we can answer on our own. We need to speak with her doctors. Agreed? Alex?"

His cousin held up both hands. "Fair enough. And about contacting your mom?"

Damn. He scrubbed a hand along his jaw. "If you want to call my mother, do it, but I have nothing to say to her. And when she does something to hurt Gran— and trust me, my mother will—it will be on your conscience."

He pivoted away to end the conversation only to find Johanna standing behind him, her worried eyes making it clear she'd overheard at least part of their exchange. He slid an arm around her shoulders. "Johanna, let's go. We need to take care of Ruby and Pearl."

The weight of Alex's jealous gaze seared his back. For his entire life, his grandmother, the ranch and time with his cousins had been his stability, his grounding force. In the span of the week, all of that was being threatened. Without his grandmother as the glue, would their family hold together?

Johanna had accused him of not understanding how she felt when she lost her whole family. For the first time, he fully grasped what she meant. The impending sense of loss left a hole in his chest. And the prospect of having his mother roll into town creating havoc did little to reassure him.

He tucked Johanna closer to his side and wondered if he could dig deep enough to keep her this time.

Johanna curled against Stone's side, resting her head on his shoulder and soaking in the feel of his fingers stroking up and down her arm. The ceiling fan in her bedroom gusted cooling air over her bared flesh. So easily, they'd fallen into old habits, tossing aside their clothes the second they crossed the threshold of her cabin.

They hadn't even discussed it or questioned it. They'd sought the blissful escape of losing themselves in each other. The ease of that unsettled her. Eventually they would have to resolve the differences that had made her walk before. The past seven months had been hell, but they couldn't just pretend the future didn't matter, even if lounging in her lavender-scented sheets with him felt deliciously decadent.

Stone kissed the top of her head, the stubble on his chin catching in her hair. "My cousins brought up something at the hospital that I can't ignore, as much as I might wish otherwise."

She glanced up at him. "What's wrong?"

"I'm going to have to tell my mother about Mariah's cancer."

"Oh, wow, I hadn't even considered that…" The last she'd heard of his mother, Jade had been living with a boyfriend in Paris. "Is she still in France?"

As best as Johanna could remember, Jade had moved in with a wealthy wine merchant about four years ago and hadn't come home since. Johanna had gotten the feeling Jade was hiding as far away from her family as she could.

Stone shook his head. "She's in Atlanta now. She went through another rehab two months ago and decided to stay near her shrink rather than go back to her fast-living wine merchant sugar daddy. Having such a large trust fund can be a blessing and a curse. Too much cash on hand to feed the habit, but plenty of money to get the best care during the next detox."

She had few memories of his mom, most of them conflicted, depending on if she was in the middle of a frenetic drug binge or somberly drained from another stint in rehab. "How do you feel about that?"

He eyed her wryly. "How do you think I feel?"

"Not happy?"

"Mariah doesn't need the drama draining what strength she has."

Johanna slid her arm around him, hugging him, her leg nestled between his. "I agree, but eventually she'll have to be told."

He nodded, his chin brushing the top of her head again. A long sigh shuddered through him. "I was a crack baby."

His stark declaration caught her by surprise, stunning her still and silent. She scrambled for the right thing to say but could only hold him tighter to let him know she was here to listen. In fact, she wished he had trusted her enough to open up before now. "Stone, I don't know what to say."

"There's nothing to say. People assume it's a poverty issue, but that's not always the case. My mother was addicted to cocaine when I was born. I didn't know that until I was an adult and saw my medical records. I just thought I needed all those developmental therapists and tutors as a kid because I wasn't as smart as my cousins." He kept skimming his hand along her back as if taking comfort from the feel of her. "My first days on this earth were spent detoxing."

She pressed a kiss to his collarbone, still too choked up to speak. Her eyes burned with tears she knew he wouldn't want to see. Thank God, Mariah had been there for him.

His hand kept up the steady rhythm. "I don't like to take medicines. I figure with a junkie mom, genetics aren't on my side as a father," he said darkly, the deeper implication clear, explaining the mystery of why he seemed so determined to deny himself a family of his own. "And what if that early addiction is still there lurking, waiting to be triggered again?"

She blinked back the tears and tipped her head to look up at him. "What does your doctor say?"

His handsome features were strained, his jaw flexing. "Not to snort coke."

She skimmed her fingers over the furrows in his forehead. "How can you make jokes about this?"

"It's better this way." He captured her hand and pressed a kiss into her palm. "I want you to understand why I'm not comfortable being a father or passing along my genes to future generations."

"Why didn't you try to make me understand before?

You have to know I would have listened without judging." Although she had to wonder. Would she have been able to accept that he didn't want children? Or would she have pushed for him to resolve his feelings in order to have things the way she wanted them?

"I thought you would run if you knew. Then you ran anyway, which only confirmed my suspicion." He threaded his fingers through her loose hair, cupping the back of her head. "Now, there's nothing to lose."

Her parents' love had been such a grounding foundation for her all her life, giving her a confidence she carried with her even now that they were gone. She'd always thought about how lucky he was to have Mariah—Johanna hadn't considered the scars he must carry because of his mother's addiction. "I am so sorry for what you went through as a baby and for all you went through afterward with your mom."

He searched her eyes. "And you aren't upset that I didn't tell you before?"

Was she? She searched her heart and decided *upset* wasn't the right word. *Disappointed* fit better. That he'd held this back only reinforced her feelings that they hadn't been ready to commit before. For whatever reason, he hadn't been able to trust her, and she hadn't looked any deeper than the surface.

She understood now that he'd never be able to give her the family she craved. His resistance was rooted in something much deeper than she'd ever guessed. But even knowing that she wouldn't be able to move them to a healthier, happier place together, she couldn't help wanting to savor this time with him. She was deeply moved that he'd trusted her enough to share this. She just wished he loved her enough to address the problem. For now though, with her emotions ripped raw, she would take whatever tenderness she could find in his arms until she found the strength to move forward with her life again.

"Not angry." She kissed him once, lightly, before continuing. "Just glad you told me now."

"You're being too nice about this." He tunneled his hands through her hair again and again in a rhythm that both soothed and aroused.

"I'm seeing things from a new perspective, questioning if I really gave you the opening to share the darker corners of your life." She took in the handsome, hard lines of his face, thinking about all the times she'd fantasized about him as a teenager. She'd idealized him and idolized him for so many years; she hadn't given him much room to be human. "I created a fantasy crush image of you and expected you to live up to that. It wasn't fair to you."

"You truly are too forgiving."

"I have my limits," she admitted. "I'm human, too."

"I should let you go, but all I can think is that someone else would take advantage—" his voice went gravelly, his arms flexing a second before he tucked her underneath him "—and there's nothing in this world I want more than to keep you safe."

"You know what I want more than anything? I want to make love to you until you can't think of any more gut-wrenching discussions for us to have." She angled up to kiss him once, twice, distracting him so she could roll him to his back. "I want us to try to be normal for a while."

"You can absolutely feel free to console me with sex."

As much as he tried to joke, she could see the raw emotion in his eyes and knew he'd pushed so far outside his comfort zone, he would need time before he could go further. So she offered him the only comfort he would allow now—an escape, a reprieve that could be found in each other's arms.

She sealed her mouth to his again. His arms wrapped around her in a flash, his hands curving around her bottom and bringing her closer. She straddled him. The pressure of his erection against the core of her was a delicious friction. Already, a euphoric haze seeped through her veins, evicting her concerns—at least for this stolen moment together.

Ten

Johanna woke to the sound of voices. Or rather one voice and a couple of different barks.

She pushed her tangled hair off her face and sat up, sheet pooling around her waist in the empty bed. Blinking to clear her mind and vision, she saw Stone's boots still on the floor, his shirt tossed over a chair. Where was his rumbly voice coming from? Maybe he was in the kitchen?

Then she heard him…from the porch. Her window was open since the night had dipped into the seventies.

"Sit…. That's right, good girl," he said, a dog bark answering.

Pearl.

"Girl, this is the last treat. You've already had four. You're gonna get sick. Yeah, Ruby, I have another for you, too. Fair's fair."

She smiled affectionately. He was sweeter than he gave himself credit for. Although with his revelations the past few days, she could understand why he was so hesitant to let down his walls and be vulnerable. His mother had betrayed him on so many different levels from the start.

The details about his birth and early years still

rocked her. It also affirmed they hadn't been ready to get married before with such secrets between them, but it heartened her that they were making progress now. He was opening up to her, and she wondered what that could mean for them as the rest of this week played out. While she wasn't ready to think beyond the next few days, she also knew they'd moved past having a one-night stand for old times' sake.

Tossing aside the sheets, she left the bed and grabbed a silky robe from a hook on the bathroom door. The sun was only just rising, but usually she would already have her coffee in a travel mug as she headed to the barn. Being idle felt…strange.

She wrapped the knee-length robe around her and padded barefoot through the living area out to the covered porch. Stone sat in a rocker wearing jeans and nothing else. His hair stood up a little in the back with an endearing bed-head look that softened her already weakening emotions. She'd missed mornings like this with him. Ruby was lounging at his feet, and Pearl slept curled up on the porch swing.

Stone glanced back at her and grinned. "Good morning, gorgeous."

"Good morning to you, too. Any news on your grandmother?" Although she assumed there must not have been any bad updates, given his happy mood.

"Amie sent a text a half hour ago. Gran's resting comfortably and will be released this morning. Alex and Amie are arguing—as expected—over which one of them will bring her home."

"I'm relieved to hear Mariah's well enough to come home. Hopefully Alex and Amie will put their competitiveness on hold for the day." She leaned a hip against the door frame, watching the low hum of activity at the lodge in the distance. She had the added privacy of a circle of sprawling oak and pine trees since she lived here. A couple hundred yards away, beyond the trees, she could hear a couple of early risers talking over breakfast. Voices and hubbub from the stables echoed from the other side of the ranch house, but everyone was out of sight.

For the most part, she had Stone to herself. "What are you drawing?"

He tipped his head for her to join him. "Come see."

She walked out onto the porch and stopped behind his chair. Looping her arms around his neck, she peered over his shoulder, surprised to find he wasn't sketching the landscape after all. He had almost finished a sketch of Pearl on the porch swing. Even only halfway done, the likeness was impressive and heart tugging. He'd captured a sadness in the dog's eyes that mirrored the sadness she'd seen in Stone's since his grandmother's announcement. He patted her hand quietly but kept the pencil in motion.

She stepped around him and settled onto the porch swing beside the terrier. She tapped the swing into motion, staying silent while Stone lost himself in the drawing. She wanted to soak up the moment and ignore the fear that this was merely the calm before the storm.

Finally, he sighed and closed the pad, looking across at her. "Sorry if I woke you."

"I wake up earlier than this for work." She reached to touch the edge of the sketch pad on the table beside him. "I forget sometimes what a good artist you are."

"The jewelry design gene in my family takes many forms," he said offhandedly.

She smoothed her hand along Pearl's back, flattening her bristly fur. "Have you ever thought about offering more input on the designs?"

"That's Amie's realm. We try not to encroach on each other's territory. The last thing we need is more competition in this family." He scratched his collar bone, drawing her eyes to his bare chest. "Besides, this is my hobby, my way of relaxing."

Her mouth watered at the flex of his tattoo along his arm and the muscled expanse of his chest. "Did you destroy the drawings of me the way you promised when we broke up?"

"You mean the nude drawings." He grinned wickedly. "What do you think?"

She wasn't sure what she thought. In the past couple of days she'd come to realize he was very good at keeping secrets and she had been very good at dodging tough subjects in the interest of keeping her fantasy alive. "Should I trust you?"

"Absolutely," he said without question. "I'm trying to make things right. And as for the drawings, I don't need any help remembering every amazing inch of you."

He angled out of the chair to kiss her with a firm, sure confidence that swirled her senses. In a fast sweep, he lifted her and settled her onto his lap. "We have about an hour before we need to head over to the house. Any ideas how we can spend that time wisely?"

She teased the swoop of bed head in his hair. "I think you may need a shower. Are you sure you don't want to hurry and help Alex drive your grandmother home?"

"I'll just leave Alex and Amie to duke that out between them."

She leaned back against his chest. She'd missed moments like this, enjoying the steady thud of his heart. "They're both so competitive. It should be interesting to watch them once their test comes. I always felt sorry for them as a kid."

"How so?" he asked. "They had everything—money, parents, a family."

Really? He was that clueless? "They had a mom who trotted them out like prize horses and a father so tied to golf and hiding from their mom they barely saw him."

"The pageant thing was a little over-the-top," he conceded.

She couldn't hold back a laugh. "You think?"

"Amie never protested—" He held up a hand. "Wait. I take that back. She complained once. She wanted to go to some high school dance and it fell on the weekend of a pageant competition."

"Did she get to the dance?"

"Nope. She won her crown." A one-sided smile kicked a dimple into his cheek. "We found the tiara in the middle of a silver tureen of grits the next morning."

"Miss Texas Grits," she quipped. "I like it. Amie is full of grit, after all." Johanna had spent so much of her life idealizing the McNairs, minimizing their struggles, feeling sorry for them on some issues, but overall envying them.

The sound of an approaching taxi pulled her attention out of their bubble of intimacy. Johanna kissed Stone quickly then eased off his lap.

She extended a hand to him. "We should go back inside before the rest of the guests saddle up for the day. I don't want to have to fight off the tourists. They'll be drooling over a half-dressed cowboy."

Her half-dressed cowboy. The possessive thought blindsided her.

The cab drove past the Hidden Gem Lodge and drew closer, as if coming to her home. Johanna hesitated half in, half out of her door. Sure enough, the taxi stopped right at her fenced front lawn. Ruby and Pearl leaped to their feet and flew off the porch, barking.

The back door of the vehicle opened and a woman stepped out, one high heel at a time. Stone's quick gasp gave her an instant's warning before recognition hit.

The reed-thin woman bore a striking resemblance to Mariah and Amie for a reason. After four years away, Stone's mother—Jade McNair—had come home.

Stone carried his mother's designer luggage into the guest suite in the family's portion of the Hidden Gem Lodge. He'd been on autopilot since the second he'd seen his mother step out of the taxi. He vaguely recalled Johanna filling the awkward silence with small talk while he grabbed his shirt and boots. His mother had said something about seeing him on Johanna's porch so Jade had instructed the taxi driver to go to the cabin rather than straight to the lodge.

His only thought had been to divert any crisis that might upset Mariah.

He put the hang-up bag in the closet and dropped the two suitcases by the leather sofa, onto the thick wool of the Aztec patterned rug. She'd certainly brought enough to stay for more than a weekend trip.

Pivoting, he found his mother standing in the middle of the floor, shifting from foot to foot under the elk horn chandelier. From nerves? Or in need of a fix? She was as thin as a bird, her skin sallow and eyes haunted but clear—her standard postdetox look. He'd seen it enough times to recognize it, and he'd seen it fall apart enough times not to bother hoping the new start would stick.

He cut straight to the chase. "Mariah needs peace, not drama. Cause her any heartache and I will throw you out myself."

Jade nodded nervously, her hand shaking as she pushed back a hank of dark hair with new threads of silver. "I'm not here to cause trouble. I heard the news about my mother's cancer from a friend."

"Are you here to make sure you're in the will?"

She sagged onto the upholstered bench at the foot of the bed. "I understand you don't have any reason to trust me, but I want to see my mother. I would also like to help if I can—and if she will let me."

She sounded genuine. But then she always did at this stage of the cycle.

"Jade, keep in mind what I said. Mariah's comfort and health come first." He turned for the door, wanting the hell out of here and back to Johanna's cabin with the dogs.

"Stone, wait," his mother called.

He stopped with his hand on the door handle. His shoulders sagged with a weary sigh. "Remember the part about no drama? The same goes in talking to me."

She stayed silent until he finally faced her again.

Jade still sat on the bench, hugging one of those fancy throw pillows women insisted on. "I'm sorry for not being a real mother to you. I regret that."

"Everyone has regrets." He understood she had to make amends as a part of the recovery process. She'd walked the steps again and again until he had the whole routine memorized. Too many times he thought she'd bottomed out enough that she'd finally begin a real re-covery.

He wasn't falling into that trap again.

She looked at him uncertainly. "What? No telling me off? Handing over pamphlets for the latest, great-est rehab center? I just finished with one of the best, you know."

"So I hear. Congratulations." Time would tell, but he wasn't holding his breath.

"You've changed," she said sadly. "You're colder than ever, something else I need to make up to you."

"I'm an adult. I accept responsibility for who I am." He put his hand back on the door handle. "Now if we're done here...?"

Her eyes welled up. "My mother is dying. Can you cut me a little slack?"

"Yes, she is," he snapped, pushing past the lump in his throat. "And she doesn't need you sapping what strength she has left."

"Maybe I can bring her some comfort," Jade said with a shaky hope that hinted at the brighter spirit she'd been during some of the better times of her life. She toyed with a turquoise cascade around her neck, a piece her dad had made for her eighteenth birthday. "I have a small window here to get things right, and I'm not going to waste it."

"You can sit by her side as long as you're lifting her spirits. If you don't do that, you're gone." That's all he cared about. And hadn't he made that freaking clear the first time? Impatience gnawed at the back of his neck. "Now what else do you need from me?"

"Keep being the good man that you are." Her eyes went doe-wide as she launched into a facade he liked to call "the good mother." She deluded herself that she had something to offer. When he was a kid, this phase had been killer because it offered the false impression that she gave a damn.

"Right." He ground his teeth together, knowing Johanna would tell him to get through this. Keep the peace. At least, he thought that's what she'd say. He'd never given his mother that much airtime to know for sure.

"And Stone? Figure out how to be the kind of husband Johanna deserves because even I can see the two of you are meant to be together. I'm going to try to help here, but I know there's probably nothing I can accomplish better than you or your cousins."

Already this was seeping into drama-land. "Mom, can we stop? I need to go—"

She launched up and grabbed his arm. "You're the only hope I have left of making my mother happy. Even though I can't take credit for the man you've become—Mariah brought you up—I can take some pride in knowing I was your mother. At some point I must have done something good as your mom."

The pleading look in her eyes chipped away at him, catching him at a time when he was already raw from all the walls he'd torn down in the past couple of days. Johanna, with her healing spirit and love of family, would want him to try. She had helped so many—human and animals—without expecting anything in return.

For Johanna, he scrounged in his mind for a positive memory with his mother and came up with, "You helped me with my macaroni art project for kindergarten."

Blinking fast, she thumbed away a tear. "What did you say?"

He leaned against the closed door. "The teacher wanted us to use pasta to create scenes for the four seasons. I was mad because I wanted to draw horses so I blew off the 'homework.' The teacher sent a note home."

"You always were a good artist and smart, too," she said with pride.

He resisted the urge to say the crack baby rehab had probably shaved ten points or more off his IQ. A year ago, he would have opted for the joke. Instead, he opted for another Johanna-like answer. "You read to me. A lot. I remember that, too."

She sat on her suitcase. "What else do you remember about the macaroni art project?"

"After we finished—or so I thought—you said it needed sparkle." The memory expanded in his mind, making him smile even now in the middle of such a dismal morning. "We went into Grandpa's home studio and raided the jewel bags. You used a citrine stone for the summer sun. Silver shavings for winter snow. Tiny amethysts and rubies for spring flowers. And for autumn, we had—"

"A pile of leaves made of topazes." She clapped her hands and smiled. "When I heard you and Johanna were engaged, I called my mother and asked her to unearth those projects from a trunk I'd stored in the attic."

"You kept the project?" Stunned, he was glad he had the door at his back for support.

"All four seasons," she confirmed. "I got them framed, to be a wedding gift to you and Johanna. When you and Johanna broke up, I just kept them for myself. They're hanging in my living room. You can come see for yourself if you don't believe me." The hint of desperation in her eyes punched away a little more of his defenses.

"I believe you. That's really nice." And it was. Keeping kindergarten art didn't make up for the past but it meant something to him to know she'd held on to the memory, too.

He didn't think he could ever see her as a mother figure. That seemed disloyal to Mariah who'd done everything for him. Photos showed his grandfather had tried to fill the void of a father figure. From all he'd heard from Mariah about his grandfather, he would have kept that up....

That thought brought to mind other unfinished business between him and his mom. He'd learned time wasn't guaranteed, so he might as well go for broke. "I know who my father is."

Her McNair blue eyes went wide. "Is that a trick question where you try to get me to admit something?"

"No trick. I did the detective work and figured it out. A DNA test confirmed Dale Banks is my biological father." He still didn't know how he felt about that. Maybe it would have been better not to know than to continue to wonder what would happen if he ever confronted the guy with the truth.

Her jaw dropped. "Dale agreed to the test?"

"He didn't know about the test. I tricked him. But if I'm right, I think he already knew and didn't want to be a father, or he refused a test in the past."

She nodded.

Stone followed the rest of the thought to its logical conclusion. "And he wasn't interested in being a parent."

"I'm afraid not, son." She stood and reached to pat

his arm, but stopped just shy of actually touching him. "I'm so sorry."

He winced at the word *son* but decided to let it slide. "Apology accepted."

Yes, anger and betrayal churned inside him, but he refused to stir up drama right before Mariah came home from the hospital.

"Does that mean I'm forgiven?" Jade asked hopefully. "I know that I can't make up for what I put you through, but I would like to know you've found some peace. You deserved better."

"I have Mariah," he said without missing a beat. "I got the best."

No more blaming the past for current issues. He had to shoulder his own mistakes from now on. Which meant he had a final confession to make to Johanna, and with his blinders off, he understood she might well never forgive him. But lying to her through evasion was no longer an option.

The sun sank on the horizon like a melting orange Dreamsicle.

Johanna drew in the sweet fragrance from the field of bluebonnets. After a full day of walking on eggshells around the entire McNair family, she was more than ready to jump all over Stone's suggestion that they slip away for a ride before supper. She should have known he would choose to ride to his favorite patch of McNair land.

She slid from her horse, leather creaking. "What a great idea to come here to watch the sunset."

He swung a leg over and dismounted. He opened the saddlebag, pulled out a yellow quilt and passed it over to her. With a pat to his quarter horse's flank, he let Copper graze alongside Johanna's palomino.

She shook the quilt out onto the ground and dropped down to sit with an exhausted sigh. It seemed like aeons ago that she'd woken up to find Stone on the porch sketching doggie portraits.

"What does your grandmother want to do about Pearl since the Montana couple reneged?" She'd been surprised when he announced the family had changed their minds, but then she'd always wondered if Pearl should stay with Mariah.

He pulled two water bottles from the saddlebag before sitting beside her. He stretched his legs out, boots crossed at the ankles. "Gran expects us to proceed as planned with the backup families once we take Ruby to her princess digs."

"Sounds like Mariah really has her heels dug in deep." Johanna sipped the water, trying not to get her hopes up too high over how right this felt with his warm muscled thigh against hers while they sat shoulder to shoulder. "I have to admit, I'm surprised. I always thought Pearl was her favorite."

"Pearl was actually my mother's dog." He tipped back his water bottle, his throat moving with a long swallow.

"How did I not know that?" She thumbed the condensation on the outside of her water bottle. "I can only remember Pearl coming to Mariah about four years ago and Mariah saying offhandedly that Pearl had been abandoned by her owner."

"That's pretty much dead-on correct," he said drily. "My mother bought her from a pet store, paid a fortune for her. Thought she was getting her own *Wizard of Oz*

Toto. Once Pearl wasn't a puppy anymore, my mom didn't want her. Too much mess, too much nipping, too much trouble to take with her to France."

"That's sad to hear." Would the little terrier remember Jade? Be confused? "Shelters are full of older puppies just like that. Thank goodness your grandmother took her."

"Just like she took me."

She slid an arm around him. Jade showing up after so long must have rattled him. "Your grandmother did a great job with you. You're an amazing man."

He didn't smile or even look at her. He picked at a clump of bluebonnets and smashed them between his fingers. "It's crazy, but she blamed herself for the selfish decisions made by her adult children. I think she saw me as her second chance to get it right after my drug addict mother and my trust fund uncle who never worked a day in his life."

"You work very hard." Too hard, in her opinion.

"She still doesn't trust me to take over the company." He sprinkled the bits of bluebonnet leaves over her lap.

"She can't doubt your skills as the CEO of Diamonds in the Rough. You've expanded the company in a tough economy." She wasn't a business major, but she knew magazines had written glowing features on him.

"Mariah doubts my humanity instincts. Something you yourself have noted, as well," he pointed out. "And that stings more because I'm not sure it's something I can fix."

"Oh, Stone," she said, her heart aching over the hurt they'd caused each other. She shifted, swinging her leg over to straddle his lap. She took his face in her hands. "I never should have said that. Whatever our differences, I know you care about people. I guess that's what frustrates me most. Your refusal to see how good you are."

Unable to take the pain in his sky-blue eyes, she leaned in to kiss him, hoping he would feel all the emotion in her flowing into him. No matter how hard she'd tried to deny it, this was the only man she'd ever loved. The only man she ever would love.

His arms wrapped around her, his hands sliding up her spine and under her long braid. With deft fingers, he worked her hair loose, combing through it until her every nerve tingled to life. In a smooth sweep, he rolled her onto her back, her legs hooking around his waist. A fresh whiff of bluebonnet perfume wafted up from the press of their bodies. Already, she could feel the swell of his erection between them. What she wouldn't give to be with him, out here in the open.

"Stone," she whispered between deep, luscious kisses, "we should go back to my cabin."

"This is my land," he growled possessively, nipping along her jaw and up to her earlobe. "No one's going to find us."

"Yours?" Her head fell back, gasping. "I thought it was all jointly owned."

"We each have a section that belongs exclusively to us. This became mine on my twenty-first birthday."

"Why did you never mention that before when we came here for picnics?" She swatted his bottom lightly. God, she loved the way he filled out denim. "It would have been nice not to worry about people stumbling upon us."

He angled away, propping himself on one elbow to look directly into her eyes. "You pegged it when you said I was holding back. I planned to surprise you on our wedding day with plans for a home."

A pang shot through her chest at the fairy tale he'd tried to give her. As much as she knew she'd made the right decision then, she'd missed out on a lot of happy moments, too. Her throat burned until she cleared it.

"I would have liked that."

"Except there wasn't a nursery in my plans."

The burn in her throat shifted, moving down into a cold knot that settled in her stomach. "You know how I feel about that, and I'm beginning to understand why you feel otherwise. I've watched you for years as you helped out the staff with games for vacationers and I guess I always thought you would change your mind."

"Liking children and being a father are two different things."

She sifted through his words, wondering what he was trying to tell her by bringing her here, because clearly he had something on his mind. "But you want a space away from here, a home in your bluebonnet field."

"I never had a regular home like other kids." He picked up one flower petal after another and placed them in her hair. "Not with my mother zipping in and out of my life. A couple of times she even took me with her when she left."

"Jade 'took' you? That had to be confusing."

"Hell, yeah, it was. Especially the time the cops stopped us at the Mexican border and charged my mother with kidnapping. My grandmother had legal custody at that point."

She searched his face, shadows making it tougher with the sun surrendering fast. "Why Mexico?"

"Easier access to drugs, most likely." He said it so

nonchalantly her heart broke. "She dodged prosecution for custodial interference by agreeing to go into rehab. Again. But if we learned anything over the years, we know that unless the junkie is committed to coming clean...rehab is just a temporary, Band-Aid fix."

She kissed him again because there just weren't any words for all he'd been through with his mother. Having her here now when he was still reeling from his grandmother's cancer news had to be overwhelming. Johanna poured all her love into the kiss—and yes, she loved him so damn much, always had, ever since she was a teenager with a colossal crush that had matured into so much more.

Groaning, he trailed kisses along her jaw, her cheek, her forehead before burying his face in her hair. "Johanna, more than anything, I want to be with you out here, just us on a blanket in my field full of bluebonnets."

"Of course, I want that, too." She slid her hand between them, palming the length of his steely erection. A moist ache settled between her legs.

"Before we're together again, we need to be sure it's forever. No more pretending we could ever have a fling."

Her heart sped in her chest like a hummingbird. "I agree."

"So we need to clear up one last issue."

The little bird in her chest sped faster. The only remaining issue had to do with children. Where did she stand and how far was she willing to compromise?

"If we make love now, we don't need a condom."

She blinked in shock, certain she couldn't have

heard him right. Terrified to hope. "You've changed your mind about having children?"

"Hell, that's not what I meant, Johanna."

His eyes squeezed shut tight for an instant before he opened them again, sapphire-blue eyes so full of regret she only had a second to prepare herself before he continued.

"There's no easy way to say this. I've had a vasectomy."

Eleven

Stone knew he'd just lost Johanna. He could see it in her eyes. Just as he'd feared, once he told her everything, it was over.

That didn't stop him from trying to hold on to her. He wasn't giving her up so easily, not this time. So he sat on the quilt beside her and waited to take his cue from her. Her whole body was rigid. She shook just a little, trembling from the aftermath of a direct hit to her tender, sweet heart.

A heart he didn't deserve, no matter how much he wanted to claim it.

She blinked quickly, her eyes as green as clover even in the dimming day. "You…you did what?"

"Just what I said, and God, Johanna, I am sorry to have to say it at all." He took her hand, her fingers quivering, and he hated that he'd brought her this pain. "I had a vasectomy right after I met my biological father, which also happened to be around the time my mother checked out of rehab early again. I knew her next fall was inevitable. And I was right."

He'd been so damn sure of himself and his choices.

Her breath was as shaky as his hand. "You were so young. You still are."

Her words echoed the mandatory counseling session he'd been forced to sit through before the surgery. It made a whole hell of a lot of difference hearing it from the woman he loved instead of a well-meaning health care professional who'd made the same speech a hundred other times. He could have never predicted loving someone so much it made him question everything he'd ever believed.

"It was way before you and I started dating. Because I swear to you—" and he meant it with every fiber of his being "—if I'd had an inkling of what having you in my life this way would mean, I wouldn't have done it."

"Have you ever considered having the procedure reversed?" she asked, each word carefully enunciated, her breathing fast and shallow. Clearly, she was holding on by a thread.

"Not until I met you."

"How do you feel now?"

"If you want a child, I will do that for you." Even saying the words scared the hell out of him, but the thought of losing her scared him more. For Johanna, for their kid, he would figure it out. He refused to fail as a parent. "But you need to understand that the more time that lapses the less chance a reversal has of working. Do you have any issues with adoption?"

She shook her head, but there was still something about her stunned expression that made him uneasy. This was too much, too fast for her. She'd barely had time to process the first bombshell he'd dropped.

He waited for her to speak but she kept looking around the field of bluebonnets, the horses grazing, the circle of trees—anywhere other than at him.

Nerves strung tight, he pressed ahead. "I have two drug addict parents. I was born a crack baby. Consider me a broken model. As far as I'm concerned, I would rather fund orphanages and adoption agencies to help babies like me that didn't have a rich grandma to step in. But if you have faith I can handle being a parent, then I'm going to trust you."

"Thank you," she said woodenly. "I understand how difficult that was for you to say."

"Then why do I still see smoke coming out of your ears?"

"First of all. It's not just smoke. It's pain, Stone. Real, deep hurt." Her hands clenched into fists, and she drew her arms in closer to herself, away from him. She kept shaking her head slowly from side to side. "But yes, there's anger, too. All those months we were together using birth control, you were lying to me, letting me believe that you might be open to having a family some-day even though you knew otherwise." She shoved to her feet, dusting the flower petals off her jeans in angry sweeps. "It wasn't just one lie by leaving out something in your past. It was a lie *every time we made love*. I'm having a difficult time wrapping my brain around that."

She thrust her hands into her hair, pressing against her head as she paced.

"Yes, it was a cop-out on my part not telling you." He stood, walking off the quilt and toward her, wary. "I'm an even bigger jackass than you imagined."

She stroked her fingers through her horse's mane, a nervous habit he recognized well. "Stone, I'm… I don't know what to say other than I feel betrayed." She looked up at him, her eyes so full of pain the clover-green was dewy with unshed tears. "How could you say you love me? How could you propose to me and keep something *this* important from me?"

"I intended to tell you, even though I knew it would drive you away. Maybe that's why I delayed because I knew it would make you leave me." Just as it was doing now. The hole in his chest widened until he fought back the urge to howl in denial. "Then it was too late. Apparently, it still is."

She turned to him hard and fast, fire spitting from her eyes. "Don't you get it? It's not that you had the procedure. That happened before we were a couple. It's because you lied to me, again and again. Telling me now… I don't know if that's enough. I just don't know."

"God, Johanna." His voice cracked as he reached for her.

She yanked away, her horse sidestepping sharply. "I can't…"

"Can't what?"

"I can't process this. I need air—away from you." She hitched a foot in the stirrup and swung up onto her palomino.

He didn't bother to stop her. There wasn't any use. His worst fear had happened, just not for the reason he'd expected. She hadn't left him because he couldn't father her children. She'd left him because he hadn't trusted in their love enough to tell her.

Johanna gripped the reins tightly in her hands even though she knew Goldie could find her way back in the dark. The evening had started out on such a hopeful note only to end in total heartbreak. She'd even chosen

Mariah's horse to ride as a tribute to the woman who meant so much to them all. Now she could only think of everything they'd all lost.

Goldie slowed from a canter to a trot as they neared the stables. And, oh, God, on the lanai, a wedding was taking place. The trees were strung with lights. Sunflowers and wildflowers filled the space, a live band played as the happy couple walked back down the aisle. The whole ranch would echo with music all night with the reception in a special barn built for just such catered occasions.

She'd dreamed of a wedding just like this.

Squeezing her eyes closed, she let Goldie find her way back to the stables. The regular scents of hay and leather offered none of the normal calm she found here in the barn, her realm. The noise level didn't help with the reception in full swing and some kind of party going on in the hot tub, too. She could have sworn she heard someone calling her name....

She looked back over her shoulder.

Amie was walking fast in a whispery sequined sun dress and cowboy boots only someone like her could pull off. Her brother trailed behind her, hands in his jeans pocket.

"Wait!" Amie waved, bracelets sliding to her elbow. "Johanna, I have to talk to you."

There was no missing the panic in her voice, which launched an echoing wave of panic in Johanna. "Is something wrong with Mariah?" She slid from her horse, her own boots a dusty, scarred contrast to Amie's shiny black leather.

Amie shook her head, her long hair in two loose

braids swishing. "No, she's fine. We just got a surprise visitor. The king—Enrique Medina—is in the lodge. He wants to save us the trouble of delivering Ruby so he's coming here." She clapped her hands, bracelets jingling. "Thank God we had the presidential suite available because every other room is booked. But he's here and he wants to meet Ruby, and Gran couldn't find you or Stone, and you didn't have your cell phones."

Alex put a hand on top of his sister's head. "Amie. Chill. Johanna's got it now. Right, Jo?"

Johanna looked back and forth between them and it didn't appear they were joking. "The king that wants Ruby is here now?"

Amie nodded quickly. "We can't keep him waiting any longer."

Johanna looked down at the stained jeans and sweaty white tank top. But he wanted his dog now. "Give me five minutes to throw on a dress and pull back my hair. I'll be right there."

She could do this. For Mariah, for Ruby, and yes, even for herself. She could pull this off. What a time to realize Stone had helped her unearth a confidence in herself she hadn't known existed.

By the time Stone finished riding alone for an hour, then brushing down Copper and returning him to the stable, he still had no clue what—if anything—he could say to Johanna to ease the pain he'd seen in her eyes. Pain he'd put there. He loved her and yet he'd still fallen short.

Music echoed from the barn on the other side of the stable yard, and from the sound of things, it was a wedding celebration in full swing. As if he didn't already feel lower than dirt. Had fate scheduled a wedding for tonight with the specific purpose of torturing him? Seeing the happy bride and groom stabbed at him with all he should have given Johanna. She wanted a family. She deserved to have the family she dreamed of. She had such a loving, nurturing heart. Would she leave here altogether?

She loved the ranch as much as he did.

He hadn't thought about that before. She'd been tied to the land in one way or another for most of her life. Just because he held the deed to a piece of property didn't negate all the heart she'd poured into Hidden Gem.

The only thing that kept his feet moving right now was the need to check on his grandmother.

He darted from the stable to the main lodge, boots sending dust puffing with each heavy step. And damn it, he'd left his suitcase at Johanna's. But he wasn't willing to push his luck with her tonight. He needed to get his head together first and come up with a plan to ease her heart even if that meant he couldn't have her back. He wanted her happiness above everything.

Except plans were in short supply as he climbed the steps to the massive log cabin–style lodge that had been his home his whole life. He should have taken a side entrance but his feet were on autopilot. Staff cleared away the wedding decorations on the lanai.

Pushing through the large double doors into the great room, he nodded to all the staff but didn't pause long enough to give anyone a chance to speak. He vaguely registered there was a frenetic buzz to the place that didn't seem connected to the wedding celebration since that was all taking place outside. Yet nothing appeared out of the norm. Wealthy socialites curled up on the leather sofas with cocktails. Older couples played poker in a far corner by the massive granite fireplace. He could hear laughter from the hot tub outside. Alex's business ran smooth as silk.

Only a few more steps and he would be clear of people, period, and into the private wing. He could shut himself in his suite with...nothing. He had nothing left and had no one to blame but himself.

A door opened ahead of him and his gut clenched at the thought of another confrontation with his mother. Instead, his grandmother stepped out on her own two feet, with a cane, but walking. She even wore clothes instead of a robe, a simple dress but complete with a Diamonds in the Rough signature piece around her neck. Amie hovered beside her, as if his willowy featherweight cousin could catch their grandmother.

Stone charged ahead. "Gran, what are you doing out of bed? You should be resting."

She waved him back. "I'm fine. The doctor released me as long as I use the cane."

Amie interrupted, "A walker. But she would only agree to the cane since it's one of our designs."

Stone felt like his head was about to explode. "Let me walk you back to your room. We'll talk over tea or something while you *rest*."

His grandmother patted his hand. "Stone, the king is here. In the presidential suite."

"Run that by me again?"

"Stone, we need to get moving," Amie said. "Enrique Medina decided he would come to us for his dog to save you the trouble. Johanna is doing the meet and greet now because we couldn't find you and you weren't answering your damn phone." She swatted him on the arm. "Now let's get moving to help her."

He glanced at Alex. "Do you have Gran?"

His cousin nodded.

"Thanks." Stone sprinted down the hall. Johanna had freaked out over meeting the Landis-Renshaw family. This was going to be way outside her comfort zone. While he knew she was amazing and would handle the meeting smoothly, he hated that she would feel nervous or uneasy, especially after the emotional hell they'd both been through today.

He passed by familiar framed landscapes mixed with photos, images of famous people who'd stayed at the lodge or worn Hidden Gem pieces. Finally—thank God—finally, he made it to the presidential suite. The door was cracked open enough for him to see Johanna sitting next to an older gentleman in a suit with an ascot. Johanna held Pearl, and Ruby slept at the king's feet. If Stone hadn't known the man was deposed royalty, he would have thought she was talking to any prospective pet owner.

Johanna had changed from her jeans into a simple white dress and matching white leather boots, her hair in a side ponytail, trailing a wavy blond cascade over her shoulder. She was pure Texas but with a designer elegance and poise, smiling and nodding at something the king was saying.

Stone realized he wasn't needed here. Johanna had it totally under control. Not a single nerve showed through. She wasn't even fidgeting with the diamond horseshoe that dangled on the silver chain around her neck. Something had happened to her this week. She didn't need him for confidence or help, and God, she was magnificent.

She glanced at the door as if sensing he was there. Her eyes lost their sparkle but she kept her composure. "Come on in, Stone, and hear the good news from our honored guest."

Stone forced a smile onto his face and stepped into the presidential suite. "Sir, we're honored that you would come visit us at Hidden Gem."

The deposed king had a reputation for being a bit of a hermit who lived in an island fortress off the coast of Florida. "I am so sorry to hear Mariah is having health concerns. It is a joy to have one of her dogs and my honor to make things easier for her by coming to her directly."

"Thank you," Stone answered, his head spinning from this day, blindsiding him nonstop. "It appears Ruby has found a great new companion."

Johanna stroked Pearl, still perched in her lap. "He also shared more good news. General and Mrs. Renshaw have decided they want Pearl after all. The three dogs will get to see each other at family reunions. Isn't that wonderful?"

A roaring started in Stone's head, growing louder by the second. Thoughts of his fight with Johanna, his grandmother's illness, his mother's arrival—his whole world was falling apart and there was nothing he could do about it. His eyes landed on Pearl and he knew. His grandmother needed to have this pup with her. Mariah, who'd given so much of herself to others, needed her favorite dog and needed someone to stand up, to make the decision to put her needs first. He would adopt Pearl so his grandmother could keep her near.

Even if it cost him the position as CEO of Diamonds in the Rough, he loved the little mutt and he wasn't giving her up.

"I'm sorry, sir." He strode into the room, boots thudding against the thick rug patterned with a yellow rose of Texas theme. He swiped Pearl from Johanna's lap before she could stop him. He cradled Pearl in one arm. "She's staying with me after all."

Standing, Johanna gasped. "But your grandmother's requirements…"

"I'll talk to my grandmother. She needs Pearl now more than anyone. I'll take care of Pearl during Mariah's treatments—and afterward." That last part stuck in his throat but he didn't doubt his decision. After seeing Johanna through different eyes this week, he'd learned the meaning of real love. His arms wrapped tighter around the dog. He nodded to their guest. "Thank you again for helping us rehome Ruby. Let us know if there's anything you need to make your stay more comfortable."

And manners be damned, the whole company be damned, Stone left with his dog, a dog that carried the scent of bluebonnets from Johanna.

As she listened to Mariah make small talk with the deposed King, Johanna's heart was in her throat.

At least Mariah and the twins had joined them so she didn't have to carry the conversation on her own, but it was the most torturous hour of her life. Not because she was intimidated by royalty—the man was truly approachable and, truth be told, she felt more confident now. But wondering about Stone was tearing her apart.

She couldn't believe Stone had left with Pearl, that he'd made such a beautiful and selfless sacrifice for his grandmother. He'd ignored his grandmother's test because he knew Mariah needed the comfort. Anyone who knew Mariah would understand she didn't make frivolous threats. Her test might have seemed strange, but she'd known what she was doing.

Johanna toyed with the diamond horseshoe pendant and realized Mariah never did *anything* by accident. She'd meant this test for Johanna, as well. The McNair matriarch had treated Johanna as a daughter every bit as much as she'd treated Stone as a son. This journey had brought Johanna the self-confidence to push Stone for the answers she needed, as well as bringing about an openness between them they should have had long ago.

She kept replaying the look on his face as he'd left with Pearl, remembering him telling her the story of how Pearl had come to his grandmother. As a vet tech, Johanna had observed countless people with their animals. She recognized true affection and a connection when she saw it. He didn't often show his emotions, but she'd seen the sketches he'd made. Stone was the right one to care for Pearl so Mariah could keep her during her treatment, and he was the perfect one to take Pearl afterward. No question, Stone loved the scruffy little pooch.

She'd already realized there was much more to Stone than the cowboy Casanova, stony facade he showed the world. Yet she'd let him down, as well, today. He'd told her his secrets, owned up and offered to make amends as best he could, and she'd panicked. She'd walked out on a man who'd been abandoned by his mother and his father. A man who was willing to give up his life's work and billions of dollars to put his grandmother's happiness first. He loved his grandmother, and yes, he even loved the scruffy little pooch enough to risk everything.

That was the man for her and she didn't intend to wait another minute to get him back.

She stood, resting a hand on Mariah's shoulder. "Ma'am, would you like some refreshments sent in or do you need to rest?"

Mariah smiled at the king with a twinkle in her eyes. "We're having a lovely visit. Refreshments would be nice."

"Perfect. I'll let the kitchen staff know." Johanna grasped the excuse to leave with both hands.

"And Johanna?" Mariah's voice stopped her at the door. "Be sure to take something to that rebellious grandson of mine."

"Yes, ma'am." Johanna smiled back at the woman who wasn't just *like* family. She *was* family.

Racing through the lodge to the kitchen, she didn't have to wonder where to look for Stone. She angled through the lanai party group in full swing, vacationers and guests from the wedding filled the place to capacity.

She stepped clear of them into the starlit night, music from the live band at the wedding reception still filling the air. Stone loved this land and she understood the feeling. The land all but hummed under her boots as she saddled up the first horse she came to—a sleek gray quarter horse named Opal. A simple click launched

the beautiful beast into motion, sure-footed even in the
night with only the moon and stars lighting the way in
a dappled path.

The wind tore through Johanna's wavy hair, rivulets
of air rippling her dress along her skin. She'd never felt
more alive and more afraid than right now. This was
her chance for everything, if she could only find the
right way to let Stone know how deeply she loved him.

Approaching Stone's favorite piece of land, the part
that belonged to him, she ducked low under a branch.
The moon shone down on Stone lying on the yellow
quilt, staring up at the sky with Pearl curled up asleep
beside him.

Her heart filled with tender feelings for the man
who'd been let down by so many, yet still had a full
heart to offer her.

Johanna dismounted. "Stone?"

"Do you know why this particular part of the land is
my favorite acre?" he asked without moving, the night
breeze ruffling Pearl's wiry fur.

She settled her horse alongside Stone's and walked
to the blanket. "Why is that?"

"The bluebonnets. They remind me of you. The
peacefulness and the sweet scent carrying along the
breeze of home." His eyes slid to her. "That's you."

She sank down beside him, sitting cross-legged.
"Stone, you take my breath away when you say things
like that."

How many times had she imagined a future with
him back when she'd been a fanciful girl? He was everything she'd hoped for and so much more. More real.
More complicated and compelling. She wouldn't trade

any part of him for the simple fantasies she'd once built around him.

"Good. You deserve the words and everything else. Whatever you want. Children. Home and hearth. Building a family. Don't settle." Even now, he fought to protect her.

He just didn't realize that she knew what was best for her now.

"I'm not settling." She wanted to reach for him but they had things to discuss first. Their reunion hadn't been a smooth, joyous coming together. It had been stilted steps toward each other because they couldn't stay away. But that was their path and she would keep on walking it. Toward her future with him. "I was hurt by what you told me today, but I shouldn't have run away. You opened up to me, and I let you down."

"You spoke the truth, though. I owe you more apologies than I can speak in a lifetime."

She hugged her knees to her chest and mulled that over for a minute, sifting through for the right words. "I guess we both aren't perfect. I tried to make you fit some high school fantasy and almost missed out on something so much better—the man you've become."

Sitting up, he captured a strand of her hair, his hand not quite steady. "Does this mean you forgive me?"

She nodded, tipping her face into his touch. "You told me you're willing to compromise with having one child—biological or adopted—however the cards land on that. I accept your beautiful offer."

He cupped her head and drew her toward him for a kiss, the closemouthed sort filled with a relief and intensity that seared straight through. "Johanna, I love you so damn much, I will do my best to be the man you deserve because, God help me, I can't live without you."

"I don't want to live without you, either," she admitted. "I've tried it. I don't like it."

"I don't want you making sacrifices for me."

"It's a bigger sacrifice to be without you." She knew that with a thousand percent certainty. No matter what the future held, she wanted Stone in her life, her heart and her home forever. He was her family.

His eyes held hers, his fingers smoothing her cheek and then tracing her lips.

"You don't know how much…" He took a deep breath and released it in a shuddering sigh. "I'll do everything I can to make this right. To give you the life you deserve."

"I know. We'll fill our home with dogs, and dote on our nieces and nephews, and yes, maybe a child of our own. But we're going to do it together."

He moved closer to her, Pearl huffing in irritation over being disturbed, then settling back to sleep. "I want to make sure you know what you're signing on for."

"What do you mean?"

"I realized tonight when I took Pearl here that somewhere along the way to being the CEO for Diamonds in the Rough, I lost sight of who I really am, lost sight of where I belong."

"And where is that?"

"I belong here, to the land, to the McNair land." He scratched his dog's ear. "I'm not a CEO who happens to be a cowboy. I'm a cowboy who happens to be an executive."

"Okay? And that means?" She wasn't certain, but

the fact that they were talking so openly gave her a new hope for their future.

"It feels crystal clear to me." He cupped Pearl's head. "My grandmother was right to give me this test. It helped me to understand. I'm not meant to be the CEO of Diamonds in the Rough."

"Whoa." She pressed a hand to his chest. "I'm completely confused."

"It's time for me to be my own man. This land, this corner, belongs to me and it's time for me to follow my destiny." He tapped her lips to silence her. "Before you think you've hitched your wagon to a broken star, I have a hefty investment portfolio of my own. And I don't see stepping away from the company altogether. I've contributed designs to the company that have landed big."

"But your plans to take the company international?"

He shook his head. "That was ego talking, the need to prove I'm better than my cousins even if I don't have parents that give a damn about me."

She reached for him. "Stone—"

"Johanna, it's okay. It's not about competing. Not anymore. It's about finding the right path. Mine is here. I want to build a home for us. Ours. A place to start our future. Not some wing at the Hidden Gem Lodge. But a place of our own to build our family."

"You have this all thought through." And it made beautiful sense.

"Even if we have a dozen children of our own, I would still like us to consider…"

"What?" she prompted.

"There are a lot of children out there who need homes, babies like I was, except they don't have a rich grandmother to pick up the pieces for a newborn going through withdrawal. It's a lot to take on. What do you think?"

What did she think? She thought this was the easiest question ever. "I'm all-in, wherever the path takes us, as long as we're together, cowboy."

* * * * *

If you loved this story don't miss
USA TODAY *bestselling author Catherine Mann's*
ALPHA BROTHERHOOD *series!*

AN INCONVENIENT AFFAIR
ALL OR NOTHING
PLAYING FOR KEEPS
YULETIDE BABY SURPRISE
FOR THE SAKE OF THEIR SON

All available now from Harlequin Desire!

She looked prettier than a painted picture come to life. Yep. Trouble with a capital *T* if he didn't get his mind back on business.

"After you learn the details of your share of the Lassiter fortune, you'll be able to buy me dinner next time." *Next time?* Man, he was getting way ahead of himself, and that was totally out of character for his normally cautious self.

Hannah looked about as surprised as he felt over the comment. "That all depends on if I actually agree to accept my share, and that's doubtful."

He couldn't fathom anyone in their right mind turning down that much money. But before he had a chance to toss out an opinion, their waiter showed up with their entrées.

Logan ate his food with the gusto of a field hand, while Hannah basically picked at hers, the same way she had with the salad. By the time they were finished, and the plates were cleared, he had half a mind to invite her into the nearby bar to discuss business. But dark and cozy wouldn't help rein in his libido.

Hannah tossed her napkin aside and folded her hands before her. "Okay, we've put this off long enough. Tell me the details."

Logan took a drink of water in an attempt to rid the dryness in his throat. "The funds are currently in an annuity. You have the option to leave it as is and take payments. Or you can claim the lump sum. Your choice."

"How much?" she said after a few moments.

He noticed she looked a little flushed and decided retiring to the bar might not be a bad idea after all. "Maybe we should go into the lounge so you can have a drink before I continue."

Frustration showed in her expression. "I don't need a drink."

He'd begun to think he might. "Just a glass of wine to take the edge off."

She leaned forward and nailed him with a glare. *"How much?"*

"Five million dollars."

"I believe I will have that drink now."

Don't miss
FROM SINGLE MOM TO SECRET HEIRESS
Available May 2014
Wherever Harlequin® Desire books are sold.